The Pride of Parahumans

Joel Kreissman

A THURSTON HOWL PUBLICATIONS BOOK

ISBN 978-1-945247-07-1

PRIDE OF PARAHUMANS

Pride of Parahumans © 2016 by Joel Kreissman

Edited by Sherayah Witcher
Cover art by Donryu
Book design by Arbor W. Barrow.

First Edition, 2016. All rights reserved.

A Thurston Howl Publications Book
Published by Thurston Howl Publications
thurstonhowlpublications.com
Knoxville, TN

Mailing address:
jonathan.thurstonhowlpub@gmail.com

Printed in the United States of America
10 9 8 7 6 5 4 3 2 1

Chapter 1

I was woken from my comfortable sleeping position by a siren blaring less than a meter away from my fairly large vulpine ears. Startled I leaped out, or at least as much as one can do so in a zero-g sleeping bag clipped onto the wall at six different points.

"Hey Silver!" came the voice of the most annoying corvid in the solar system out of that same intercom as the horrid wake-up call. "Get your Barbie-doll ass out of bed. We're coming up on that rock soon."

"Seriously Cole? That again?" Under my breath I muttered, "At least I don't have a cloaca." If the uplifted raven heard me, he gave no sign. Slightly more annoyed than usual, I started wriggling out of my insulated cocoon to the door of my cramped cabin. Pausing before the mirrored surface of the metallic door I noticed what Cole had so lovingly referred to as my "Barbie-doll ass".

Grabbing onto one of the handhold bars distributed all throughout the ship, I rotated in mid-air and spread my legs apart so I could see the reflection of what lay between them. That is, a bunch of black fur with white guard-hairs like the rest of my body, hence the nickname "silver", but if you looked close enough you might spot my anus, and if you looked really close you could see the opening of my urethra. "Barbie-doll ass"–please, I look more like a plushie or one of those non-humanoid animals in Japanese anime. Yes, you read that right, I have no genitals. The twisted corporate bioengineers who spliced human and fox DNA together and extruded the resulting transgenic slush over a calcium-titanium alloy skeleton did not see fit to print me a set of reproductive organs. The vast majority of parahumans had some variety of genitalia even though the geneticists had made sure that they were sterile, but I was part of an experiment of some sort to see if workers who couldn't waste valuable company time screwing one another functioned more effectively than those who did. It turned out that we did not. Without the extra testosterone or estrogen from a set of gonads it seemed that we were less motivated than those who had semi-functional ovaries or testes.

Okay, we were downright lazy. They could have asked anyone who owned a neutered dog or cat what happens when you surgically excise an animal's motivation and saved themselves a few million bucks.

Anyways, introspection over, I flung myself out the door and into the corridor. I wasn't going to bother with clothes until I knew whether they wanted me to go outside. It wasn't like I've got much to hide anyways.

As I was floating up the corridor to the bridge, I felt a paw slap me on the rear and propel me into a bulkhead. Looking back I saw a meter-and-a half tall red panda wearing a set of workman's coveralls trying to catch himself on a handrail with his ringed tail. Denal, our mechanic.

"The hell were you thinking?" I snarled at him getting increasingly annoyed by the second. "Doing that in the middle of a wide open hallway? In zero gravity?"

"Hey, Argentum, you dress like that and you have to expect some workplace harassment." He was joking of course. When you can't make babies and have practically no diseases the corp crèche supervisors don't bother to instill taboos about sex. It was practically expected for co-workers to hold orgies in the break rooms, now that we actually had breaks. I couldn't see the appeal of it–me and Denal had had sex once or twice but all I felt was a pain in the butt that made it impossible to sit for half a week. Thank the corps for using us in microgravity. I shrugged it off and darted for the hatch to the bridge.

I should probably explain the name I gave myself–Argentum, or "Argen" for short, is ancient Greek or Latin or something for, well, silver. I know, original, but I'm a chemist by training and during my accelerated education I found myself wondering why so many elements had symbols entirely unrelated to their names. There is neither an "a" nor a "u" in gold, or for that matter silver doesn't have an "a" or a "g". So I did a bit of research in the crèche library and found that scientists like to name things in long-dead languages that nobody speaks anymore. After discovering the full names of certain metals in those languages I thought they sounded cool. What? I was barely three years old.

The bridge was a cramped space for a room intended to accommodate multiple people attempting to maneuver in zero-gravity. There was barely enough room for the four of us to stand and just slightly more space to secure ourselves with straps. Flight chairs and data terminals jutted from every wall. Cole and Aniya were already there. Cole was a raven the size of a large turkey, albeit with a much bigger head. His wings were also modified with small claws at the ends, apparently a small atavism the bioengineers found that dated back to the earliest birds from the time of the dinosaurs. They enabled him to hang onto an overhead handlebar while his feet manipulated the flight controls. Apparently there was a prevailing theory among some of the corps that created us that creatures that evolved in a three dimensional environment would be better suited to navigating the depths of space than us terrestrials. So rather than adding some animal genes to a human baseline genome like most did for their deep space workforce, they took the genomes of dolphins, parrots, octopi, corvids, and seals–basically any aquatic or flying animal that showed a decent level of intelligence-and boosted their brainpower until they could operate a spaceship. I don't know how well it worked but I do know that for all his annoying quirks, Cole was a great pilot.

Aniya couldn't be more different, she was a rescue taur. A four-legged, two armed centauroid of mixed human, wolf, and possum heritage designed for both heavy lifting in the low-gravity mines out here in the Belt, and bailing out fellow workers whose suits sprung leaks. Above her waist she looked like a lot of parahumans, anthropomorphic torso covered in black fur with a lupine head, but below she looked like one of her natural kin, except considerably larger, like the size of a fully grown horse. And a peek under her pressure suit would reveal a bit of her possum genome, a prehensile (but mercifully still furred) tail and a pouch big enough to accommodate an adult human or most parahumans. Yes, a nice soft pouch modified to seal airtight around a small hose that would supply a distressed miner with oxygen until he calmed down, all safe and warm in a secure pocket of flesh...Oh dear I was rambling, wasn't I?

Right, so there I was on the bridge with the rest of the

crew of the nameless prospecting ship we'd managed to get a hold of sometime after the combination of violent raids on corp bases and legislative action on the behalf of sympathetic lobbyists that won us our freedom. The monitors were displaying several different views of an asteroid a couple kilometers in diameter that our scanners seemed to indicate held a promising concentration of mass. The plan was simple, latch onto the rock, toss out Aniya and whoever happened to draw the short straw with a load of mining equipment, prop up a burrowing mass driver over the mass, and drill until it got within a few centimeters. Then they'd chip off some samples, I'd analyze them in my lab, and if the mass was something valuable, we'd dig it out and take it back to Ceres for sale to one of the local fabricators or the freighters supplying earth with needed minerals.

"We should arrive in a little more than half an hour," Cole announced to the rest of the crew. "Better get ready." Knowing his tricks it was more likely we'd be there in fifteen to twenty minutes. Whichever unlucky bastard had to go with Aniya wouldn't have much time to suit up.

Aniya glanced at me and Denal and shrugged. "Might as well get it over with." She pulled three straws out of her suit pocket with her right hand while she held onto a rail with her left. She grabbed one straw in each of her free semi-prehensile forepaws so that they all appeared roughly the same length. Cole flapped over and took the one in her hand before flying back to his console, leaving me and Denal to take the ones in her paws. I looked at the one in my hand and it was barely five centimeters long. I compared it to Denal's, and his was a full cm longer. Dismayed, I floated over to Cole–sadistic corporations–his straw was seven cm.

"Guess I better get dressed," I said dejectedly as I let the losing straw fly off. Aniya plucked it out of the air and put it back in her pocket. Then she held out a foreleg and drew me close to her. She bent over and looked down at me with an amused expression on her wolfish face.

"Come on, I'll let you sleep in my pouch tonight if you don't complain too much." So maybe going out on that exposed hunk of rock wasn't so bad after all.

For once, that avian bastard gave us the correct time to arrival. I spent fifteen extra minutes standing in the airlock wearing the light pressure suit that was sufficient for parahumans of my model to survive in the vacuum of space. One of the perks of being built rather than grown is that we have a much greater tolerance of low pressure than humans do. If necessary I could remain conscious in hard vacuum for up to ten minutes, more than enough time for a nice rescue taur crewmate to drop her pants and shove me in her pouch, but I wasn't going to take any chances. Space is a harsh, unforgiving environment, and under the supervision of the corporations we lose ten percent of our number every year. I don't know the mortality rate now that we're free but I would bet pretty good odds that it's still rather high, definitely above birth rates now that the corps aren't popping a thousand of us out of the tanks every quarter. We used to have two full time miners, but then Billy ignored the warnings of an incoming radiation storm and got his brains fried. His share of that haul bought us a 'bot with enough sense to scurry for shelter at the first sign of cosmic rays.

There was a series of jarring lurches forward as the harpoons pulled us down to the surface of the asteroid and anchored us there. The airlock opened and the ramp lowered as we made our way down to the regolith. Aniya gleefully bounded across the landscape carrying some 500 kilos of equipment while I drove a rover with the really heavy stuff. Conceivably the two of us could carry the mass driver between us, but neither of us was experienced enough with maneuvering in microgravity to risk doing so while bouncing around. After half an hour of that we arrived at what our radar indicated was the shallowest point above the mass concentration we were interested in.

As we unpacked, I prepared a portable spectrophotometer. Unlike the clunky devices of the 20th century, this device was little bigger than a suitcase, including a specialized computer for interpreting the data. I scooped up a sample of regolith and poured it into a sample cuvette that I inserted into the machine, and within a few minutes the device had exposed the asteroid dust to every wavelength of light known to mankind and its creations, contrasting the reflections with those given off by baseline samples stored internally. Once I'd analyzed the readouts, I addressed Aniya subvocally using the implants in our throats. No point wasting breath when some subtle movements of the larynx would do.

Looks like basic nickel-iron. Maybe a little heavy on the iron but not exceptional.

In my experience certain metals tend to aggregate around iron, came the wolf-possum's sub-vocal response. *Some of those are worth quite a few qcoins if I am correct.*

I'm not saying that it isn't valuable-if nothing else we could try to sell the coordinates to one of the big haulers.

Ooh, almost lost your bedmate you asexual dog.

Did you intend to subvocalize that Denal?

No, sorry. Not really.

I cut the horny Asian raccoon off of my channel. Seriously I thought pandas were going extinct from lack of sex or something. I tried not to think of his commentary as I helped Aniya set up the burrower. We set it up more or less exactly above the masscon, whatever it was, and switched it on. The drill bits at the bottom of the machine dug into the asteroid and every few minutes a rock was magnetically accelerated out the top, pushing it slightly deeper in and flinging the fragments far out of the way. Every hour or so I opened a hatch to siphon off some dust for analysis. After the first hour all I could see was an increase in the iron content, as well as some minute quartz and agate crystals. The second hour I noticed the dust was starting to reflect more light between 570 and 590 nm in wavelength.

Don't get too excited, I told the others still linked to my comm channel. *There's a lot of things it could be, likely just some pyrite.*

"I'm still going to be looking up the price," Cole couldn't use subvocal comms like we did, something about the avian voice box being much differently shaped than the more-or-less human ones we had. "Just in case you're wrong."

And I think it's time to turn this thing off and dig in by hand and paw. Aniya turned off the mass driver and pushed it over. She then began to shuffle around in the dust with her forepaws, looking a bit like a baseline dog burying a bone.

I picked up a rock-hammer and inched towards the two-meter wide hole. *I need a large sample for a density index*, I explained as I attempted to pry out a rock that looked like it would weigh maybe two kilograms. Once I had it loose I carried it over to the rover where I calibrated a balance to the minute gravity of the asteroid and weighed the rock. Quite a bit more than 2 kilos...promising. Then I did a few laser scans to determine the stone's exact dimensions, which I then plugged into my suit's computer with a series of blinks and bites on different teeth oriented to various keys. I saw the results.

Well, it could be gold, I subvocalized, *or maybe platinum, or lead.* Gold was one of the most discussed elements in the Belt these days. When the corporations had started to mine the asteroids the price of gold had sunk to levels unseen in human history. But when the revolution occurred, gold prices soared above the peak they'd reached during the early 21st century economic recession until the parahuman colonies decided that they'd be exporting minerals to earth and the price started to decline again. Currently it was hovering somewhere around 50 Cerean qcoins per gram. Not quite a fortune, but still a significant amount of money for a small mining outfit like ourselves. I personally didn't understand why the humans thought it was so valuable. Sure there were some chemical and electronic applications for it, but the market value couldn't account for those practical uses alone. I could understand why platinum was worth more, though. A lot of life-support systems used it in catalytic converters. Still, lead was worth something, too, a lot of habitats built radiation shelters out of it. I signaled the excavation bot to unfold and prepare to bring up the pieces of the masscon.

The spider-like robot walked over to the site on four spindly legs and positioned itself over the hole where Aniya was digging. As she exposed the concentration of mass that had drawn us to the asteroid, a four-pronged claw lowered itself on a winch down the hole. She guided it over one of the larger exposed stones she had drilled out of the asteroid and signaled for it to pull up. As it walked over to the rover I stole a glance at the piece of rock it had pulled out. Though mostly grey stone, I could see a few spots where the yellow metal shone through. There was a lot of it, three big rocks and dozens of smaller ones– a total of almost a quarter of a metric ton once we'd taken off most of the worthless silica and iron. Over twelve million Ceres qcoins worth of gold. We might even be able to pay off the mortgage on our ship.

If we had known the trouble those rocks would bring us, we might have just left them there.

Chapter 2

It was dark. I could feel myself enclosed on all sides in sticky wet mucus and veined flesh. But I didn't feel scared or alarmed, rather I felt calmed by the encasing pressure, safe and secure. I moved myself deeper into the flesh pocket as I felt the gentle massage of my host's pulse. Normally, Aniya would only allow the use of her pouch for emergencies, but she knew about my...eccentricities, and she allowed me inside her fairly often. I had been in there for barely an hour before I was thrown out of my serenity by a loud siren interspersed with Cole's frightened screeching.

"Everyone to the bridge, we've been hit by laser fire. I repeat, we are under attack!" I could feel Aniya jump off her bunk and propel herself down the hallway with me still inside her pouch. It must have looked odd to anyone watching, a fat half-naked wolf taur with a second tail sticking out from under her groin—which was covered by a pair of taur-sized panties, you perverts.

"What is going on?" It felt strange to hear Aniya's voice echo through her body like that. The extra pair of lungs in her lower body allowed her quite the reverb.

"About a minute ago something fried one of our aft sensor pods. There wasn't any indication of a radiation storm and I picked up a heat signature 200 kilometers in that direction. So I took us behind the nearest asteroid." Cole's voice carried none of his usual jocularity. He was truly scared. "Where's Argen? zie is better at reading these sensors."

At that moment I felt a hand grab my tail.

"Found zir," came Denal's voice as he yanked me out of the pouch. I burst out in a cloud of mucus and reached around to grab him for pulling me out of my hiding place, making sure to coat his fur in a nice layer of pouch slime. He cringed at the feeling and let me float there next to Aniya's backside. "Makers, for an asexual being you have some odd kinks, Silver."

"Later." I did not feel inclined to explain, for at least the tenth time, that I did not consider my fondness for the interior of my crewmate to be sexual. Though to be honest I sometimes wondered if my adrenals did provide enough hormones for a proper sex drive and my brain redirected it somewhere away from my lack of traditional reproductive organs.

Anyways, I wiped my hands off on Denal's coveralls and jumped over to a tablet to call up the sensor logs. Sure enough, they showed a heat signature following us since we left the asteroid where we had picked up the gold chunk. Unfortunately, it didn't tell me much. It seemed we hadn't bothered much with active radar on that side of the ship, and now we were completely blind in that area thanks to our pursuer's precision shot. "Worthless, we need a better view of them to even know what we're up against. Can you try sending a drone out to the edge of the rock we're hiding behind?"

"Yeah, yeah, sure I'll launch one." Denal tried to avoid putting himself in contact with the slime I'd left on him as he went over to his console. We had half a dozen survey drones that Denal would frequently send out on arcs around asteroids we thought looked promising. They'd circle the rock a couple times, playing their radar over it and taking snapshots of the surface in multiple wavelengths, and transmit it back to our ship, saving a lot of time on prospecting for ores. He shot one out to swing around the asteroid we were currently using for cover and programmed it to scan outwards rather than at the asteroid. Meanwhile Aniya and I called up manual controls for our primary collision avoidance coilguns. Hitting a stray rock with a fast-moving iron slug tended to get it out of the way a lot faster than melting it with a beam of concentrated light, and anyways lasers were a bit out of our price range.

The drone reached the far side of the asteroid and transmitted back a view of the region of space beyond. Radar imaging finally brought me a view of what I had been looking for in the first place–a small (relatively speaking, we were about twice as large thanks to the need for mining equipment and landers) cargo ship covered with laser turrets and a pair of long tubes that I had no reference for. It didn't seem to be moving as we scanned it. "It's like it's just waiting to see what we do."

Aniya had the first suggestion. "Maybe they're moving when we're not watching. Why don't we send the drone back out to see if they've come any closer?" Denal punched in the commands and the drone flew back out to take a second look. It hadn't moved–however, there was now another smaller and much faster object moving out towards us.

"Incoming missile!" Cole screeched as the object swung around the asteroid and headed straight for us.

Panicked, I switched the auto-tracking on my turret back on just as Aniya did the same. Registering the small, fast incoming object as a collision threat, the automated systems sent streams of darts at the missile. Mere seconds from impact one of the darts ruptured the missile's fuel tanks and triggered an explosion that took out the explosive weapon entirely and sent shrapnel flying everywhere–thankfully not fast enough to do much damage to our ship.

I didn't understand how they had been able to lock onto us from the far side of an asteroid, but before I could think of something another missile came in from the opposite side of the previous one. Aniya just barely managed to shoot that one down as well. Noticing the drone following the missile, it came to me. "Denal, shut down the transmission to that drone! They're tracking it!"

The panda switched off the transmitter, then as an afterthought he shut down all of our transmitters just to be safe. Now we could see nothing of the attacking ship. Until either we or the apparent pirates moved to the opposite side of the asteroid we were blind.

"Now what?" Denal asked, evidently a bit scared now that we had just barely escaped death twice. I thought it was obvious–we wait for the pirates to get bored and leave. Unfortunately, that wasn't the case, and after half an hour of sitting there the enemy ship came up around the asteroid and began to approach us. As it drew nearer, I saw that our attacker had decided to bolt on oversized engines and a pair of docking arms onto their miniature freighter. Seeing how that sort of craft rarely needed to dock with anything but a full-sized spaceport, I doubted they had peaceful intentions.

I panicked again. Hastily aiming the gauss turret I was

controlling at the pirate vessel I blasted away with a stream of iron. I saw a docking claw tear itself off and fly out into space, a laser turret shatter into a million shards of glass, and then there was a puff of gas out of one of the holes I made in the main hull of the ship. But it still kept coming at us.

"Move, move, move!" I urged to whomever would listen.

Cole swung our ship away from the asteroid, and the pirate ship continued on in the same direction it had been following the whole time. Of course, there being no friction in space you needed to fire retro-rockets in order to slow down before you hit anything, which didn't bode well for the crew of that ship. Either their control systems were damaged, or, as suggested by the gas vent I'd opened up, they were dead.

"I'm not picking up any signals from them," Cole stated as he moved the ship in for a closer look. I called up a spectroscopic analysis of the cloud streaming out of the ship–approximately 80% nitrogen and 20% oxygen, with traces of carbon dioxide and other trace gases. Plus, ice crystals of a reddish-black fluid that appeared to contain a significant concentration of iron.

I dropped the tablet in shock, not quite the effect it has in gravity as it just hung there suspended in mid-air. "I killed somebody," I exclaimed in horror, "it's blood. I didn't just rupture their crew compartment, it actually hit somebody."

Cole pulled up some schematics of the enemy ship based on what we could see of it. "One person space truck, designed for short hops from one asteroid to another. Pilot sits in a polarized plexiglass bubble. You got lucky."

"Lucky?" Denal exclaimed. "Do you know what the Cerean directorate does to anyone who kills someone?"

"Seizure of all assets and fifty years hard labor?" Aniya suggested. Everyone who lived full or part time on Ceres knew the basic penalties for criminal acts. "But zie was acting in self-defense. They launched missiles at us."

"They don't care, there's nothing in the laws to make exceptions and the computerized judging systems follow the laws to the letter." This information about the consequences of my rash actions sent my adrenal glands into another overdrive, but since there was no one to fight this time I instead prepared for flight, right into Aniya's pouch, shoving her into the nearest wall. As she yelped in surprise Denal continued, "That's not going to help, she's just as guilty as you are as far as the judges are concerned. For that matter, we all are."

"Crap," I murmured from inside the wolftaur's nice and safe belly as I pulled my tail in behind me. With such severe penalties, I wondered why that guy in the other ship had even bothered to attack us if he knew what was in store for him. "Any idea what drove that guy to try and kill us?"

Cole ruffled his feathers in a way that might have been a shrug. "I heard talk of some extremists who wanted us to break off trade with earth. They apparently nuked some freighter docks on the east side a while back. Trying to annihilate anything that was of more value to earth than to the Belt."

"I've seen nuclear detonations before," Aniya's voice reverberated down to her pouch. "They were a lot larger than the explosions those missiles produced when we destroyed them." If anyone could have seen them at the moment I might have rolled my eyes.

"Nukes don't have nuclear reactions when they're ripped apart by high speed projectiles," I told her in a rather matter-of-fact way. For some reason when I said that her pulse dropped slightly. "However, if they were carrying fissile material it would have set off a radiation alarm."

"But chemical explosives have barely any effect in space. They might open the hull or disable the engines, but the gold in our hold would be recoverable. And that's worthless except for exportation, so wouldn't they want to destroy it?"

Denal snorted loudly enough for me to hear it. "Then maybe he was just a plain old pirate. They do say that banditry or violent theft is the second oldest profession after all."

"And what, dare I ask, would the oldest profession be?" Aniya asked him in response. He said nothing, or at least nothing that I could hear, but I had a decent idea of what he had in mind.

"So what are we going to do about the draconian Cerean law enforcement that would have us all back in chains?" I asked my co-workers and friends with whom I had apparently committed the worst criminal offense out of necessity for our lives.

"Nothing," Cole suggested. "We make no mention of this incident and pretend we obtained this haul with no unusual troubles. Odds are he wasn't from Ceres, probably one of the smaller and more lawless asteroids. There's no way he could get away with fencing pirated goods back home."

"I could probably cover up the laser damage," Denal threw in his own contribution. "Those sensor pods are modular anyways, I could simply remove the remainder of the attachment and recycle it. Then weld over the hull scars to make it look like micrometeor pitting."

"Well, I guess that's it then. We're safe." Yet strangely, despite my words, I did not feel any more assured. I curled up tighter in the rather appropriately named fetal position.

Chapter 3

We arrived at Ceres without further incident two days later. Sure enough, Denal had managed to conceal the evidence of our skirmish with another ship fairly easily. The sensor pod turned out to have taken the brunt of the damage and was easily enough detached and smashed to cover up the melted instrumentation. We jettisoned the melted pieces and stowed the rest for recycling once we got back to the manufacturer, might as well not pay full price for a replacement. The few scars on the hull were scratched over with chunks of rock from our cargo hold to simulate meteor impacts. Still there was a sense of apprehension as we disembarked from the ship and passed through station security at the second largest port on the biggest dwarf planet in the asteroid belt. Nearly two hundred thousand parahumans called Ceres home, the biggest concentration of our kind in the solar system. There were even a couple humans, mostly trade reps or ambassadors attempting to write out some manner of treaty with the Directorship.

Government out in the belt varied a great deal. Most of us had been accustomed to rule by whatever corporation had fabricated or bought us and we had little experience governing ourselves. While most human children were taught how their government worked in childhood and how to participate in it, if they were among the lucky minority to live in a democracy, we had to figure out how government worked on our own, involving a lot of trial and error. Asteroid habitats vary from direct democracy to fascism, and everything in between. In the case of Ceres the corporations had used the planetoid as a base of operations in the belt, and naturally several different corps had constructed their own processing plants and even regional administrative offices. Because few humans were willing to travel several months out to the asteroids, or more importantly sign the legal waivers disavowing their employer of any legal responsibility in the case of their gruesome demise, many of the administrative tasks ended up being performed by parahumans.

The result was that when the revolution won us freedom from the corporations, Ceres already had a vast bureaucracy running things fairly smoothly. The highest ranking administrators of the different corps, once the humans had been killed or shipped home, all got together and decided to change the various "human only" rules their corps wrote so that they applied to parahumans as well, and they otherwise set up shop like their former owners had done save that they now paid their workers. After a couple months of trying to handle a payroll of several thousand on a system intended for a few dozen, they laid off half their employees. However, they also allowed the "black market" that had inevitably popped up to operate in the open and in fact focused their layoffs on the merchants and hobbyists who they had a fair idea were earning an income on their own.

These people were allowed to rent shops in the common areas of the habitats, cutting out some administrative costs and giving the Cerean Directorship, as the conglomeration of ex-secretaries called themselves, an additional source of income besides the money from exporting their extracted minerals to earth. In addition the layoffs left the Directorship with a sizeable fleet of surplus spacecraft that they no longer had the manpower to operate. They were going to scrap these vessels until some bright manager came up with the idea of offering some of the laid off miners loans to buy the extra ships. You can probably guess which category Aniya, Cole, Denal, and I fell under. So yes, not exactly the best system of governance ever, but we had one of the lowest crime rates in the belt, or so the propaganda–sorry, "public relations"–department claimed.

Anyways, that brief history of Ceres does not do justice to the wonder that is the market caverns. As the corps mined out the dwarf planet they dug huge holes miles beneath the surface in order to get to the largest concentrations of mass in the asteroid. These tunnels were a minimum of two meters tall to accommodate the miners and their equipment, but the caves that had held the most valuable minerals often reached five meters in height and a football field or two in length or width. Since there was plenty of pre-existing living space in the worker barracks and tunnels, many of these caverns had been reinforced with long titanium columns and filled with multiple levels of storefronts. The .028 gravities made it easy for most people to simply jump from one level to another through holes in the rickety paneling placed in front of shops so the customers had something to window browse from. It's rather incredible, in a ramshackle slum kind of way.

This day the others and I were leaping about the asteroid's interior, carrying the remains of our destroyed sensor pod in three separate bags and headed for a dealer we had looked up on the asteroid's local network. We found them in a three-floor warehouse on the east wall of the cavern, alongside a number of other shops that sold spacecraft parts. One would think those would be located near the docks, but Directorate rules were that any merchants not working directly for the Directorate itself had to reside in the market caverns. At least they had delivery services and installation teams. We found a sales rep, a heavy set spider monkey hanging from the ceiling racks by his tail, and dumped out our collection of parts.

"Well," he stated as he picked over the remains with all four of his primary limbs. "It looks like you beat this up rather thoroughly. You say a meteor did this?"

That was our story and we were sticking to it. "Yes," I replied.

"Surprised your point-defense didn't stop it. You guys looking to replace that too?"

Denal offered an explanation seemingly spontaneously. "Our computers glitched, the start-up program for the auto-guns was omitted from the command queue. We managed to fix that, though."

The salesman snorted derisively. "Computers, nearly two centuries of use and those humans still haven't figured out how to make them work reliably. We don't sell ship grade computation materials or programs, but I could give you some recommendations." Denal took a list of stores with decent electronics on his wrist device. He probably wouldn't actually buy anything but the gesture would throw off suspicion. "Anyways, you probably want something a bit sturdier than these factory-standard sensors. I happen to have some brand new pods with carbon nanotube reinforced superstructures, fresh from the fabricator. A tad pricey, but I could give you 8-15,000 qcoins worth of store credit from these parts."

"How much?" I asked somewhat skeptical.

"Oh, about 105,000 Ceres qcoins," he said.

"So that's what, 90,000 to 97,000 that we'd need to pay?"

"I think you may have misunderstood me. That's with the best estimate of the credit you get from these parts. Normally they cost 120 k."

That price was practically obscene. We had convinced the representative from the Directorate's exports division, which they held a practical monopoly on, to part with 10.8 million qcoins for the gold we had offloaded at the docks, but we still had to pay back over 35 million of the loan we had taken out to buy our ship from the Directorate, plus several thousand a month for routine maintenance and fueling.

He must have noticed the expression of disbelief on all our faces because the sales rep spoke up then. "Tell you what, you must have at least five more sensor pods like this covering each major surface of your fine vessel. I'll give you the replacement and trade in all your other pods for 600,000 qcoins."

I did the math quickly. "So you're saying our intact sensor pods are worth just 21,000 apiece, is that it?"

He held all four palms up in an open-handed gesture of surrender. "They're long, obsolete, and most likely pretty banged up from all the flying around in this big field of flying rocks. You're not going to get a better deal than that."

I kind of doubted it. Technological progress in the belt was nowhere near as fast as it was on earth, and there was little demand for spaceship sensors on earth so most likely our pods were less than two cycles out of date even after more than a decade in operation. "I'm thinking more like 500k," I retorted. "These can't be that much better."

"580,000. They really are, both ten times more durable and fifty times better resolution than those old things of yours."

"530. I can tell the chemical composition of a gas jet at ten kilometers with enough resolution as is."

"Okay, five hundred and fifty thousand Cerean qcoins and that is my absolute final offer."

"Fair enough." I keyed up my own wristpad's wallet to transfer 550k to the store's account. We'd still have a bit over ten megs to pay towards our mortgage once the monthly expenses had been paid. I felt somewhat satisfied that I'd been able to negotiate the price down so low. Normally these things went much less smoothly.

Naturally, we got the first indication that things on Ceres were about to go wrong just as we were leaving the cavern. We spotted a holographic poster of a ferret in a pilot's vacuum suit under the words "Missing, information related to the disappearance of this subject will be rewarded." In smaller print the hologram elaborated that the subject had taken out a sizeable loan from the Directorate to purchase one of their short-range transports approximately a week ago. Three days ago the signal from his ship went silent. This sort of thing wasn't uncommon, the shifting orbits of the asteroids made some signals difficult, but something told me this wasn't an ordinary space trucker. I checked the model of the ship he had bought again. Sure enough, it was the same model that had almost killed us two days ago, though it usually didn't carry missile tubes or security-grade lasers.

"You think that was him?" Aniya walked up behind me and put a hand on my shoulder as she asked the obvious question that we were all thinking at that point.

"Maybe," I replied. "What I don't get is why all the fuss over some guy who probably just ran off on his loan." Aniya shrugged and we continued on to the tunnels that would take us back home to our ship.

We got our answer the next day as our new sensor pods were being installed by a team of monkeys and rams. As I was running one of the new pods through its paces with a hand tablet plugged into a socket on the base of the pod and looking at the ceiling in every spectrum the thing could handle, one of the rams doing heavy lifting came up to me. "Hey, you hear about that weasel who went missing?"

"I saw some holo-posters," I stated as nonchalantly as I could manage.

"Well, they say he was a clone of some Directorate bigwig and that he hadn't gone dark for two days before daddy had those posted along all the tunnels in the planet." I looked at him in disbelief. A clone? Those were rare luxuries. It cost hundreds of thousands of qcoins just to operate the bio-fabricators used to make them. It would explain though why he had been so foolish as to attack a Cerean vessel. Not only did he have an influential relative who could conceivably cover his tracks he was most likely less than five years old, that being when we had managed to petition the United Nations of Earth for the right to replicate ourselves. And just because we came out of the vat fully grown didn't mean that we were born mature. At 28 I pretty much considered myself to have been a complete idiot before the age of eight. Yet the laws treated us all the same whether we were two or thirty-two years old because that had been how the corporations had treated us and the Directors had been lazy. I tried to smile at what I presumed to have been meant as a joke by the technician whose ass wasn't possibly at stake and hurried through the remaining checks. I did not bother to test the other pods but instead bounded back inside the ship to discuss the new situation with my crewmates.

When I told them, Denal and Aniya just stood there with a glassy look in their eyes and their mouths hanging wide open. Cole wasn't particularly surprised. "Should have known it would be one of those fresh from the tank rich morons."

"So what now?" I inquired. "If we did kill him and the Directorate finds out, I think forced labor until the days we die might be a light sentence."

"We fly," Cole flapped his wings, knocking me and Denal off our feet in the low gravity. "We fill our helium-3 tanks and pick another asteroid that won't turn us over to our new corporate masters."

"Sounds like a plan," I said. "But which rock might that be?"

Chapter 4

We spent the next three hours going over the map of the surrounding asteroids and looking up the local wiki's entries on the inhabited planetoids our ship could reach from Ceres at this time. Juno was ruled out–they had an extradition treaty with the Directorate and a history of complying with their demands. Iris didn't, but they operated under a government that seemed the closest to the human system known as "fascism" known to the Belt. Hygiea, with one of the largest direct democracies since ancient Greece, initially looked promising, but then we saw that the majority of the population were strident pacifists and not even point-defense guns were allowed. I couldn't imagine that they would like us very much.

"What about this one?" I pointed at a large spherical planetoid, similar in size to Ceres. It was near the edge of our range.

Cole looked where I was pointing. "That would be Vesta, either the second or the third largest asteroid in the entire belt, depending on who you ask." He ruffled his feathers a bit and looked away. "I don't think so."

"Why, what is wrong with it?" Curious, I started to call up the wiki's information on Vesta.

Cole turned back towards me and stared. "I went there

once, about six years ago. It was anarchy, I was almost assaulted a couple times. Some guys tried to pounce on me and when I flew out of the way one pulled out some sort of jury-rigged gauss gun and told me to toss over my possessions. Fortunately for me it short-circuited when he tried to fire a warning shot."

Seriously? I hadn't known there were places where the crime rate was so bad. What kind of government would allow such a thing? I read the information I'd pulled up on Vesta. Gravity: .025 g, orbit: 3.63 earth years, population: ~50,000, government:…

"There's no government?" I asked, confused. How could a society even function without any sort of government? Apparently not well judging from Cole's testimonial. But then I thought I saw something right below the tab that read "Government: N/A". It stated: "danger level: low to moderate." I was confused.

I opened a more detailed description and jumped to "crime and other hazards". I read on.

…The ration exchanges created by the Repairman's in 2090 led to individual shortages of calories and needed nutrients. In desperation many residents turned to preying on their fellow parahumans, both figuratively in the form of stealing rations or other belongings to be traded for rations, or in rare cases literally in the form of cannibalism. The introduction of the Vestan qcoin later that year helped alleviate the starvation as the Guild began to accept them instead of food, but crime remained high until the formal establishment of the Protector's Guild in 2092. The Protectors would, in exchange for a modest monthly fee, do everything in their power to defend the person and possessions of their customers, and if

their defenses and any personal ones carried by a customer were defeated, they hunted down the aggressor and enacted restitution from them. In 2094, the Protector's Guild fractured into several competing organizations that still work to keep the peace in Vesta. Many of the most prominent Guilds offer "Guest plans" for visitors...

I looked away from the article and back to Cole. "Judging from this article you got there just a year too early. They've got something called "Protector's Guilds" now that provide security and got their danger level downgraded to moderate-low."

"And what's stopping these "Guilds" from turning us over to the Directorate?" Denal asked.

"Who says they can even do that? They're not a government or anything." Aniya interjected. "If they're like a business that just offers protection plans, the worst they should be able to do is cancel our coverage. And the article mentions "personal defense", which seems to imply that they don't mind people defending themselves, which is all we did wasn't it?"

"All right, fine. We'll put it to a vote," Cole stated. "Everyone who wants to take their chances on an uncivilized rock with no government to speak of, raise a hand." Me and Aniya raised our hands immediately. "And all opposed?" We put our hands down and Cole raised a wing claw. We all turned to stare at Denal, whose paws were firmly gripping the handholds along the edge of the table.

"Well I don't know," Denal protested, "it sounds like Vesta might be safe from the Directorate but the way you made it sound it seems like the Protector's Guilds or whatever are just barely holding things together."

"Look, why don't you go over to the bank and pay them nine million qcoins towards our loan. Think it over on the way there and back. I'll get us filled up with Helium and reaction mass so if we still haven't decided where to go we can at least reach someplace to refuel and set out again." Cole flapped away from the table and to his own pilot's perch.

"Nine million is a lot." Denal started to inch towards the door. "What if they get suspicious as to why I'm paying that much at once."

"Tell them that we don't want to be tempted into spending all that on something stupid," I suggested. He bounded out and closed the hatchway behind his ringed tail.

Less than an hour later Cole was just finishing up the refueling procedures as Denal came hurtling up the docking tube. He panted, out of breath as he shut and locked the airlock doors tight. "What happened?" I asked, looking up from the wiki entry on some frontier asteroid that would need at least two fuel stops to reach.

Denal righted himself and began to explain. "As I was coming back from the bank I noticed a security inspection team gathered near one of the ships by the entrance to the port. I asked a nearby officer what that was all about and he said that they were checking all the ships that had been in the sector where that executive's clone had vanished. He said that they were only asking if anyone had an idea of what had happened to him but I didn't like the way some of them looked." He jumped into his chair and started strapping himself in. "I would definitely say that my vote is now "yes", let's go to Vesta. Like right this instant."

I strapped myself down and signaled for Aniya, down in the equipment bay, to do the same. Cole resigned himself and signaled to traffic control his intent to depart. "We read you. The way out is clear, but why so quick to leave? You just got back in."

Cole improvised as he started to pull us out. "Oh you know," as if that ever convinced anyone, "just made it big on our last trip. Thinking we might be able to afford a down payment on a better ship this time."

"Really?" The traffic controller was still on the line. "And just where did you say you got all that *aurum*, anyways?"

Crap, maybe he was with security, in which case he could direct some of security's cutters to intercept us before we even got half a kilometer from dock if he suspected we were involved in the situation somehow. Cole spoke again, "Trade secret, if we told anyone the location our secret mine would be bled dry in a week."

"You know, you can't keep other miners from jumping your claim unless you file it."

"And since when has registering a claim stopped anyone?" I spoke up, before remembering that while the output was on speakers, the input was restricted to Cole's headset. Cole repeated my statement after looking at me odd for a minute.

"Well, suit yourself. Hope you strike big again." We were out. For now we were safe.

Once we were ten kilometers out, I unstrapped myself and walked over to Cole's station, the acceleration providing more "gravity" than Ceres had. "So how long until we reach Vesta?" I asked him as I leaned around his crash chair to look at him.

He faced me and said simply. "Ten days."

Ten days, a bit of a long trip by our standards. "Guess I'd better go and settle in, then."

The next day I finally had some time to work on my hobby. While my training had been in dead rocks and minerals, I was interested in the far more complex chemistry of living things. A large portion of the section of the ship that had been allotted to my work space was taken up by a variety of different laboratory instruments that had nothing to do with my official job on the ship, and quite a bit of the stuff I actually needed could be used for bioengineering, too. Fortunately my lab is in one of the few parts of the ship that has something resembling gravity–the room rotates on an axis perpendicular to the ship's engines. When the ship is under burn the room stops moving so that the "floor" is oriented towards the drive so that the acceleration provides gravity. When the ship is coasting, the room spins so that the samples within stay at the bottom of their containers. Sometimes I found it ironic that a place that contained at least four centrifuges was itself in a centrifuge. To get in or out, the giant centrifuge had to be stopped temporarily, which upset the samples if prolonged for too long, so I would jump in and trigger the motor to start back up again before I was even through the door all the way.

The room was dominated by a large refrigerator, a glass door and several compartments inside that maintained their contents at different temperatures ranging from slightly above zero degrees Celsius to under 50 below. A set of cabinets held a spectrometer that could just as easily be used for living or non-living samples, a miniaturized Polymerase Chain Reaction thermocycler, a

DNA sequencer, and a wide assortment of various micropipettes, pipettes, beakers, flasks, test tubes, and heating elements. Water, unfortunately, had to be brought in a large carton, there was no plumbing.

This particular day I drew two sets of four petri dishes from the fridge, one set with several spots of white or blue bacteria, the others covered with a green algae. I carefully lifted two blue colonies from each of the bacterial plates and suspended each colony in a separate microfuge tube of solution. I separated the cells in each of these tubes from the DNA they held via microfilters and centrifugal force. I then transferred the fluid to new tubes and added a mixture of enzymes, salts, and fluorescent marked primers to the solutions. Then I placed the tubes into the rack in the thermocycler and set it to run a five hour cycle.

While waiting I scooped a teaspoon of algae from each of those dishes, and placed them on a hot pad for ten minutes. Once they were dried out I tasted a bit of each sample. None of them tasted particularly good. My bacon-flavored nutrient algae apparently still had a long way to go.

After I had finished the impromptu test of the algae I'd modified I decided to wait out the remainder of the PCR cycle reading some science-fiction novels from the 20th century on my tablet. It astonished me how humans dead for so long could be both so prophetic and so wrong. Naturally, there were five minutes left on the timer when someone decided to interrupt me. I felt a rather jarring vibration along my jaw signaling that someone was trying to contact me on my subvocal comm and I bit down on my right to answer.

Who is this? I demanded feeling a bit annoyed.

It's that "horny panda", as you call him, came the reply. I swear, Denal's subvocal pickup is as obnoxious as his real voice. *There's something I want you to see. Come up to my cabin.*

I've already seen your genitalia, several times. I remembered the lab coat, goggles, mask, gloves, and pants I had just put back on in anticipation of the continuation of the experiment. *And I just got dressed again, I'm not taking this stuff off now.*

What? Oh, you're in the lab, aren't you. Denal actually sounded surprised, almost like he had something different in mind this time.

Yes, and I'm in the middle of something that could potentially shake the Belt like nothing since the revolution. That wasn't completely true, to be technical about it. The machine would hold the samples at a stable temperature until I came to retrieve them if I had to leave, but all the unsecured lab equipment I had lying around before I performed that last step of the analysis would go floating around once I shut down the centrifuge to step outside.

I'm serious, Argentum. I noticed something about our trajectory and I think we may be off course.

He'd used my full name. That could mean he was serious. Or it could just as easily mean he was dedicated to this particular joke-slash-attempt to get into my pants. *Since when do you know anything about astrogation?* I cut off the call with a hard bite on the left and popped the lid to the thermocycler.

I drew each sample into the sequencer, the fluorescent tags attached to the replicated DNA strands allowing the machine to determine almost the exact code of each based on the size of the strands and the different colored tags attached to different bases in the tagged primers. When the sequences were displayed on my tablet, it confirmed my suspicions. When I was designed the geneticists deactivated several genes related to gonadal development. The result being that I could never develop testes or ovaries. It could have gone either way given how my cells were a mosaic of XX and XY karyotypes that were otherwise identical. Presumably another set of genes influencing the development of gonads was responsible for our universal sterility. The corporations never revealed the exact genes that they had manipulated to induce these changes, but I intended to find out. I had stored my own genome, plus those of my three crewmates, in the form of plasmid libraries. The human genome was public record, so I was going over every gene known to be involved in reproduction and determining which genes made us unable to have babies. And possibly a way to make a set of junk for myself if I felt so inclined. There were plenty of organ printers available in Ceres so there should be some in Vesta.

Denal was waiting for me when I exited the lab, he was holding a tablet out for me. "Look at this," he said, pulling up a map of the Belt. "We're following a trajectory that takes us far from Vesta." A line showing our course appeared and passed the tag marked VESTA by several thousand kilometers.

"Have you asked Cole about it yet?" I inquired of him.

"I called once and he shut off his intercom," Denal replied. "He said he was taking a nap and not to disturb him."

That sounded a bit suspicious. "We should go wake him up," I said. The two of us floated over to Cole's cabin. The door was locked, but Denal was able to easily bypass it with just a couple of jump wires.

The damn crow was nestled in the cubbyhole he used as a bed when I found him, his head tucked under a wing like a stupid chicken. I grabbed him by the other wing and yanked him out. He awoke with a start. Now, Cole may have had sharp talons and a beak, but I had solid bones and they were almost 50% solid titanium, so I was strong enough to break all his limbs and wring his uplifted neck before he could give me more than a few gouges that were easy enough to patch in my lab.

"Where are we Cole?!" I shouted in his bird-brained face. "I've seen our trajectory, we're not going to Vesta."

To his credit he didn't bother with lying this time. "We're on a course to an ice asteroid, about three thousand kilometers spinward of Vesta."

"You know that raw ice is shitty reaction mass," I snarled, my vulpine genes making themselves known. "If we are lucky the contaminants won't blow up our engines."

"I'm not going back to Vesta," he insisted.

"Either we go to Vesta, or this fox is having fresh poultry for breakfast." I wouldn't really eat him, though if we did try to extract reaction mass from a dirty snowball and it ended up leaving us stranded I couldn't make promises.

He reached for the intercom with a wing claw and pressed down a button marked "voice control". "Autopilot, alter course and take us to Vesta. Most direct path from current location."

The ship's computer responded in seconds. "Calculating… warning, insufficient reaction mass. Along suggested course we will fail to reach Vesta by 147.2 kilometers."

"Then we call in a tug, that's why we retained most of

a million qcoins isn't it? Unexpected expenses?" I gave the corvid a toothy grin, he confirmed the course, and I let go of him. Then I left the room to confirm that he had in fact set us along the right course this time.

As we headed for the bridge, Denal turned to ask me something. "So, what were you working on anyways?"

I shrugged. "Trying to figure out a way to give myself genitals."

"That's great," the panda said in response. "So what's it going to be, pole or a hole? Or maybe both?"

"Currently I'm thinking that I'd rather be male."

"What?" Denal looked aghast. "You know that I'm straight, don't you?"

I smirked in response. "Why do you think I want to be a guy?"

Chapter 5

We were able to reach Vesta's primary docking port despite the lack of fuel on our part. I did indeed call a tug boat to bring us in, though traffic control charged us quite a bit for the tow—one hundred thousand Cerean qcoins. As we were brought in, I realized that the transaction could probably be traced back to us and used to locate us on Vesta. I decided we'd want to exchange our qcoins for Vestan ones or some sort of commodity currency and open a completely new set of accounts. While we couldn't convince Cole to move in immediately, he did agree to check it out for a couple days. That would give us time to decide whether or not we should stay, and if we decided to leave it would allow us to refuel and resupply before moving on to the next habitat.

As soon as we were within range of the Vesta network, I contacted a money exchange and traded our 900,000 Ceres qcoins for 700,000 Vestan qcoins. Apparently Vestan coins hadn't been mined for as long as their Ceres counterparts and thus were worth significantly more due to their lower quantity. Next I called up the webpage for the Protector's Guild whose service area encompassed the sector of the port and many of the surrounding markets, and according to the reviews I found they were one of the most thorough in their guardianship of their customers' property and wellbeing. When I saw that they offered group plans and required a live video consultation, I called the rest of the crew up. I transferred the page to the large bridge monitor and opened the link to the video chat. The screen was filled with the visage of a female cat of some kind, fur shaded grey with thin black stripes, wearing a green business suit and sitting at a desk in front of a full-wall window overlooking a city that might have been one of Ceres' smaller districts.

She looked up from the tablet in her hands and spoke to us. "Good afternoon, my name is Jessica and I'll be your agent for the Marquez Guild. Shall we get started?"

We indicated our affirmation and introduced ourselves, one by one.

"Now then, you want a group plan?" We told her that was the case. "All right then. To start with are you affiliated with any Guild, company, or government?"

"No," I replied. "We are freelance prospectors, though we did work with the Cerean Directorate most of the time." She scrawled this information on her tablet, tapped a few things that we couldn't spot, and then her eyes widened and her ears turned to press themselves against her cranium. That did not look good.

"Very well," she forced her face back into the friendly expressions she had been wearing when the conversation had first started. "What is the purpose of your visit to our fine habitat?"

Pretty much all of us showed our shock and worry at this question. Cole's tail feathers fanned out, Aniya's hackles raised underneath her shirt, Denal grabbed his own tail and started wringing it nervously, and I could have sworn that my tail doubled in diameter when the fur stood up. Thinking quickly I said, "We got bored in Ceres, wanted to see what some of the other asteroids were like."

Denal threw in "Not much excitement."

"Thought the Directorate exports guy was stiffing us," added Cole.

Finally Aniya threw in, "charged too much for life support."

Jessica tapped a few virtual keys and spoke to us again. "Your rate is calculated at 2,000 Ceres qcoins a day, rounded up to the nearest day. As long as you are on Vesta and within our service area, our surveillance network will keep track of you and automatically deploy armed drones if you are attacked." A map of the habitat with multiple areas covered partially or completely in green appeared on the screen by her image. "Be advised that if you try to leave the habitat without paying your bill we operate a number of photon and kinetic turrets situated around the docking bay."

I threw something else in before she could terminate the connection. "We already exchanged our qcoins for Vestan ones."

She looked at me and tapped something else on her tablet. "Then that shall be 1,200 Vestan qcoins per day. Same rules and conditions apply. Shall that be all?"

I nodded. She ended the call. Though honestly I was a bit curious, the difference in price was considerably greater than the exchange rate I had seen earlier. Did the Vestans prefer their own currency so strongly? I suppose it made some sense given how long the light speed delay made transactions that used servers not physically located on the same asteroid. After all, that was why so many habitats had their own distinctive qcoins in the first place.

When the tug finally towed us all the way into dock we first refilled our reaction mass and then we all left to check out the habitat. We had to see if it was still as bad as when Cole had been there. The market cavern on this asteroid was practically right next to the docks, and it took barely a minute to walk down there. It was much like those on Ceres, except that there seemed to be very little in the way of urban planning in this cave. Shops and fabricators were intermingled with townhouses and restaurants. In fact, it seemed like nearly all of the buildings were used as places of residence, or rather people had set up shop in their apartment complexes. We could tell which were businesses and which were simply dwellings only because most of the stores and fabricators had small signs on their front doors. I noticed that most had a symbol of some archaic tool, a compass rose or a hammer or a sword or something, accompanied by an odd sign that looked like a pair of inverted chevrons with a short squiggly line a little ways above them.

After browsing the slapped together city for nearly an hour and seeing no signs of criminal activity, Denal suggested we check out one of the areas not covered by Marquez. "If this section is so crime-free with one of the highest rated Guilds keeping the peace, we should see how the other Guilds handle things."

We had some doubts, but his reasoning seemed solid. We headed to a side cave that was outside the Marquez Guild's service area. The tunnel leading into the cave was unusually wide and the ceiling varied in height a great deal. At one point it was 2 meters high but just half a meter further down it went up to 3 meters tall. I was passing under one of those high ceilings when I felt what seemed like a ton of bricks landing on top of me. Still in shock, I felt a pair of hands lift my head up and press a sharpened blade to my neck.

"All right you newbs," I heard a hoarse voice from on top of me. "Hand over your wristpads, tablets, and anything you may have bought at the market. Or missy here is going to look like a *red* fox if you get my drift."

I saw Aniya and Denal turn around to stare blank-faced at me and my attacker. Cole simply flicked his eyes upward to glance at the ceiling. I got the impression he was doing the avian equivalent of rolling his eyes. "And here you were saying that the Protector's Guilds kept everyone safe here."

The high-altitude mugger on my back reared up, pulling his knife away from my throat, and laughed. "The Houses don't cover the tunnels you stupid newbies. It's all for your-"

PFFEW PFFEW

I heard some quick bursts of compressed gas and the mugger slumped over. Moving quickly, I threw him off and got to my feet. On the ground behind me was a large rat parahuman lying limply on the ground like a rag doll, his eyes wide open. Sticking out of his neck I spotted a pair of red feathered darts. Denal made a surprised squeaking sound and I turned to see what he was looking at. It was a pressure pistol, seemingly hanging suspended in mid-air.

No, not suspended, there was a shape nearby that was colored the same as the cave wall behind. It moved slightly and became a canid woman dressed head to toe in a chameleon suit. As we watched she holstered the weapon and pulled the hood off, revealing that she was a grey wolf with close-cropped hair.

"Well, hello there babe." Denal began but was silenced by a threatening finger pointed in his direction by our camouflaged savior. She walked past him to the rat she had downed and started collecting her darts.

I watched her do her work for a few seconds before speaking to her. "Thank you for saving me like that. Miss?"

She glanced up at me to answer my query. Instead she flashed me a comm number on her wristpad which I entered into my own in conference with the rest of my crewmates. *Olga Wolf,* I heard in a soft voice resonating through my jawbones. *I'm an investigator for Guild Wolf. Yes, I know, creative name.* Even through subvocals, I could discern the sarcasm.

Why are we using subvocalization? Aniya asked before anyone else came up with the idea.

Because the tetrodotoxin in those darts doesn't always paralyze their sensory neurons. Came Olga's response. *It mostly goes after voluntary muscle control, including the diaphragm. Only reason he hasn't suffocated to death is the oxygen retaining modifications our designers added.*

I picked up the would-be mugger's wrist and put two fingers to the inner edge. Sure enough there was a faint pulse, but I couldn't hear any breathing. *Why are you so concerned about being heard by this guy, anyways?* I asked her.

Oh, that. Well you heard him, I'm not supposed to be here. Thanks to some pissing match between mom and old man Jerome, the tunnels are supposed to be neutral territory. But this guy has been preying on not only newcomers like you but our own clients who have to use this tunnel to get to and from the spaceport. She walked towards Aniya and Denal and drew her dart gun. *So here's what you're going to do. One of you is going to take this gun, you're all going to take this waste of biomass back to the Marquez side, and you're going to report to the nearest Marquez officer or drone that he attacked your friend here and you shot him with an open-source dart shooter that you printed off before coming on board.* She held the gun out grip first to see who would take it.

Aniya took the gun and looked at the inexpensively 3D printed weapon a bit apprehensively for several seconds before stuffing it into one of the pouches on her tauric pants, barely leaving a bulge. *Are you sure they won't mind us pumping someone full of deadly poisons? I would have thought that the Protector's Guilds would take a bit of offense to people doing that sort of thing.*

Olga suppressed a snort as she reattached her hood. *Why, is that why you left your old place?* Everyone's eyes widened a bit at the half-joking accusation. *Oh, well Vesta was founded mainly on the principle of "you can't tell me what I can't do", so you'll generally find that people here wouldn't care whether you tipped your darts with cyanide. And anyways, the Guilds operate like insurance—the more you do yourself the less they have to pay.* She finished fastening her hood and reactivated her camouflage. I could still see a bit of an outline as she started to walk away.

But then I remembered some minor thing that she had mentioned. *Wait, you said something about "mom" and an "old man Jerome". Who are they?*

The silhouette paused for a few seconds. *I'm a clone of Georgia Wolf, the Guildmistress of Guild Wolf. Jerome Marquez is the Guildmaster of the Guild you guys are paying.*

"Does everyone on this rock have two names like a human?" Cole threw in his own comment. The rest of us glared at him for failing to remember that we were not speaking aloud to preserve the secret identity of the part-time vigilante we had here.

No, just those who are part of a clone family have last names.

Often it's the first name of the line's founder but some, like my oh so imaginative mother, come up with completely new names to add on to their own. Also many of the Guildmasters have multiple clones. The SPPS gives them discounts for some reason, I've got five sisters and Jerome has eight sons. The shadow that had saved our possessions and possibly our lives then ran off back down the way we had been headed.

I walked over to the immobile rat still lying there in the middle of the hallway. I thought I saw one of his eyes twitch a bit. So I went up to his head and flipped my kilt up, giving him a brief view of my featureless crotch. "I'm no 'missy' you scumbag," I told him and then grabbed his left hand and started pulling him back down the way we had come by his arm. Aniya came up to pick up his legs a few seconds later.

We did as Olga suggested, dragging the thug up to the nearest agent of Guild Marquez and telling him the story she had given us. He entered the information into his wristpad and asked Aniya to see the gun. She produced it, he looked it over, and then he handed it back satisfied that it was indeed an open source design that could have come from anywhere.

"You should have told us you were armed," he informed Aniya after giving her the weapon back. "We would have adjusted your rates accordingly." He then bound the mugger's hands in zip-ties and injected him with the antidote to the tetrodotoxin. We left before he fully regained his mobility.

On the way back to our ship we bought a load of feedstock for our on-board fabricator. Most spaceships intending to operate more than a day or two out from a habitat had at the very least a multi-material "omni-printer" that could make a variety of items from a number of different plastics and metals and even some basic electronics. There were even a few well-equipped ships that had nanofabricators imported all the way from earth that could construct anything from a pizza to the latest model of augmented reality contact lenses. We just had an omni-printer with a couple of robotic armatures for assembling the parts as they came out of the printer. My lab had a chemical synthesizer for automatically mixing whatever non-solid compounds we needed and a variety of microbe cultures for producing biological substances.

Cole elected for an exact copy of the pressure dart gun Olga had given Aniya. I'd engineer a plate of bacteria to make tetrodotoxin to fill the darts with. Denal, of all things, wanted a Chinese longsword with a stylized pair of procyonid's paws on the hilt. I didn't think he even knew how to use a sword but I queued it up anyways. I decided on two weapons: a spring-loaded stiletto with a blade that popped straight out of the hilt rather than flipping out–if I got jumped like that again I figured I could pull it out and slam the side of my fist into the mugger and pop the blade into his flesh–and a gun. A number of designs were now public domain so I selected a steel semiautomatic handgun that dated back almost two hundred years but seemed to still be popular. I assembled many of the parts myself but allowed the armatures to make the bullets, which were filled with gunpowder mixed by the synthesizer. As I slipped the finished weapon into the printed plastic holster I now wore on my belt I hoped that I would never have occasion to use it.

Chapter 6

We spent the next three days touring the habitats in Vesta and asking people what they thought of the present situation on their asteroid. We went to market towns like smaller versions of Ceres, hydroponic farms, and manufacturing districts, and generally got the same stories. Many told us that the Protectors had drastically reduced the crime rate, and some other immigrants from different asteroids stated that dealing with them was preferable to most of the governments they had previously lived under. We weren't accosted by anyone else, though. Whether that was due to the Guilds keeping the criminal element under control or to the weapons we were now openly carrying, I do not know. Regardless, I got the impression that many of the people we asked weren't telling us everything.

Eventually, we pieced together the story of Vesta's controlled anarchy. After the revolution, the inhabitants of Vesta, which had extensive mines and worker barracks but minimal supervision, decided to embrace the concept of no rulers. The nutrient algae vending machines were hacked so that anyone could add their biometric data to the system and receive a daily allotment of calories from the machines. The fabricators were open to use by anyone who felt they needed something. If there was a shortage of fabricator materials or some of the life support systems began to malfunction or the algae went bad someone would fix the problem. If someone went crazy and started killing people they figured that an angry mob would drag him to the nearest airlock.

Inevitably this turned out not to be the case. Air scrubbers crapped out, leaving entire sectors unlivable at a rate that overwhelmed the few people who had the initiative to fix them. Infected algae were ignored until the food became toxic, and psychopaths found ways to murder people with no witnesses to form mobs.

The tipping point came, ironically enough, when some people who were concerned about the degradation of the habitat organized and began working to fix the various problems full-time. This group, known as the Repairmen's Guild, initially suffered from a lack of manpower in resolving all the broken pieces of the habitat, until they came up with the idea of offering their members extra food rations. At first, this extra food came from algae trays and hydroponic farms maintained by the guild itself and voluntary donations from grateful civilians. But as time passed, they needed more and more workers, and many Guilders assigned to collect donations started using physical force to intimidate people into giving up their food. This led to many people becoming malnourished, and some resorted to stealing food from others. During this time, the Protector's Guild formed, and refused to aid anyone who didn't "donate" to them, and even more people starved as a result of them taking yet more of the food. Some people tried to avoid giving away their rations by offering resources they had mined, items they had fabricated, or services they could provide. After some initial incidents, the Guilds decided that they would accept payments other than food rations, which convinced many people to find things that they could produce.

Eventually, so many people were producing products and performing services that they formed guilds of their own and began exchanging products or services for those produced by others besides the Repairmen and Protectors. At some point people started giving written promises of a future good or service instead: "This file is redeemable for one kilogram of carbon from Phil" and such. And then people began to trade these promises around. Unfortunately they were easy to copy, and there were disputes as to who had the valid file.

One group noticed this phenomenon and noticed that many other asteroids used qcoins that were nigh impossible to counterfeit. They obtained a set of quantum servers and formed a guild that began trading promise files for freshly mined qcoins. The issue of starvation was largely solved. Many people even started growing plants imported from Earth or raised small animals for sale, increasing the general food supply, though the algae vending machines remained open for those who could not afford other foodstuffs.

Despite all this, theft remained a bit of a problem. The focus had just shifted from algae rations to other products they couldn't afford but still desired. Thus the Protector's Guild expanded until their organization became unwieldy and was divided into several smaller guilds.

As great as the system that had emerged spontaneously from the chaos was, there were evidently still some problems.

"What do you mean by 'We can't buy from you'?" Denal demanded from the representative of the Marquez habitat's industrial fabrication guild. The red panda was practically in the rep's face, leaning across the desk.

"It's guild rules: we can only accept raw materials gathered by one of the miners or chemists guilds," the mixed breed dog parahuman replied, nonplussed by Denal's particular way of asking him questions.

After deciding that Vesta was, in fact, safer than most of the other asteroids in the immediate area, we bought a long-term coverage contract from the Marquez Guild and set out to find uncommon minerals in the surrounding rocks. After a week out in the black, we came back with a load of tungsten, a very dense and strong metal used in a lot of heavy-duty construction work. Normally we could get a decent price for it, but now we were finding it a bit difficult to offload on the locals.

"And just why can't you accept ores from independent miners?" Denal propped his drooping upper body over the desk with his arms as he asked further questions that I was sure would not get us closer to making money from this particular venture.

The dog stuck behind the desk paused for a few seconds as if having difficulty thinking of a good reason for the rule. "Well, for one thing, we don't maintain the equipment needed to determine the purity or even identity of the product. The miners' guilds do."

Okay, now I was feeling a little offended. "I analyzed that ore," I threw out before the bureaucrat in front of us. "It is ninety percent pure tungsten. I guarantee it."

He turned slightly to face me. "And what is your guarantee worth, madam, er, sir, er…?"

I hate it when people don't recognize that I have no

gender. "I'm pretty sure the word is "zir". I'm neuter. And the name is Argentum, like the metal."

"Yes, well, Argentum, is it? How do I know that your assessment is accurate without certification from a guild? For all I know, you're lying outright about the contents of those containers that you and your colleagues want to sell me."

I grabbed my head in my left hand and started rubbing my forehead in exasperation. "At least the Ceres Directorate had their own mineral composition team," I mumbled to myself at what I was sure was a barely audible level.

Denal pushed himself up off the desk and started for the door. "So, what, we should try selling to the miners' guild instead?"

"No, I think you misunderstood me," the fabricator's rep said. "The guild as a whole doesn't buy materials; they only license and certify. You have to join the miners' guild."

As we left the office Denal and I noticed a large animated advertisement on the side of a building. It showed a view of the city around us, but the buildings were decayed like they hadn't been maintained for decades. It seemed deserted. A caption stated "VESTA, 2300 A.D." Then a figure in a pressure suit was seen walking down an alleyway. His species was indeterminable but appeared primate in origin. He walked into a house. The interior was covered with dust that he left a shuffling trail through. Entering the bedroom, one noticed a bluish metal parahuman skeleton, with the distinctive skull of a feline, lying on the bed. The figure picked up a wristpad the skeleton was wearing, dislodging the remains of the owner's hand, and sent the bones clattering to the floor.

The figure flipped his visor upwards to examine his prize, revealing the furless face of a human being. Words appeared at the bottom of the display and began to move slowly upwards, "EVERY YEAR, HUNDREDS OF PARAHUMANS DIE FROM VIOLENCE, EXPOSURE TO HARSH ENVIRONMENTS, AND DISEASE. UNLIKE MOST SPECIES, WE CANNOT REPLACE THOSE LOSSES WITHOUT TECHNOLOGICAL ASSISTANCE AND CONSCIOUS EFFORT. OUR PEOPLE ARE HEADED FOR EXTINCTION."

Then the scene began to shift, subtly at first but becoming clearer and clearer. Dust vanished, broken shelving was restored, and burnt-out lights came back on. "BUT WE AT THE SOCIETY FOR THE PRESERVATION OF PARAHUMAN SPECIES BELIEVE WE CAN REVERSE THAT TREND." Finally, the human picking over the bones of long-dead parahumans disappeared, and the skeleton was replaced by a sickly-looking, but live, panther. Then the door opened, and another panther who could have been a copy of the one in the bed, just healthier-wait, not healthier, just much younger-came through, carrying a tray of foodstuffs. The old cat smiled as he saw his clone (for surely that was what the other feline was) place the tray on a cabinet next to the bed and pull up a chair.

Then the scene shifted to a factory setting, a row of cylindrical glass tanks with robotic arms within laying flesh and sinew over metallic bones inside the tanks. It panned over to a tank with a nearly complete male red fox suspended in the tank while a team of technicians and another male fox, this one with grey hairs spotting his fur, stood nearby. "OUR CLONES ARE NOT MERE LUXURIES. THEY ENSURE A FUTURE FOR ALL PARAHUMANITY."

"Tugs at the heartstrings, doesn't it," I said as the scene started to repeat before me. Denal nodded in agreement.

"Hey, didn't that Olga Wolf babe say that she was a clone?" I thought back to our first day in Vesta. She had said she was a clone of the guildmistress of Guild Wolf, no less. And there was something else…

"She claimed that something called the 'SPPS' gave discounts on clones to guild leaders," I recalled. "Think this is the SPPS?"

Denal shrugged. "Seems likely." Then he paused as if in contemplation. "Hey, maybe we should all get clones. We can be like one of those human families. Me and Cole can be the dads, Aniya can be the mom, but what would that make you?"

I snorted derisively. "Save it until we have enough money to actually buy clones. I doubt they would charge a bunch of prospectors fresh from Ceres anything less than full price. And last I checked, clones were expensive."

"Right, right. Let's go find a miners' guild then, shall we?" Denal held up his wristpad to look up the local listings for the various guilds. Instantly, I was reminded of the video, and the titanium alloy bones falling away from the prying hands of a future human looter.

Denal pulled up a map to the dense-metal miners' guild main office, and we walked down there in five minutes. On the way, we called up Aniya and Cole and told them to meet us there. Cole was already perched on a street light outside the building by the time we arrived, but

Aniya took an extra three minutes to trot up. Once everyone had shown up, we explained to the others the guild rules that kept us from selling our ores and how it seemed that the only way around them was to join a guild, like the one we were standing outside of.

"Sounds like a stupid rule," Cole said from atop his perch above the walkway.

"He said it was because they didn't have any analysis equipment," I explained, "which makes some sense as a cost-cutting measure. But he also said that he didn't trust my own assessment. Why should being in a guild make me any better at telling the difference between tungsten and lead?"

"I don't know, why don't we ask them?" Aniya motioned towards the door. I figured we might as well see what they had to offer and pressed the intercom button by the door.

There was a buzz and the speaker clicked on. "Hello?"

I answered, "Is this the Dense Metals Miners' Guild?"

"Yes. Do you have an appointment?"

I hadn't thought of that. "No, were we supposed to make one?"

"It depends on what you are after."

"We would like to join."

There was a brief pause; then the speaker crackled again with a response. "Well, then, I've got the application forms here. I can show you through the process." The doors opened and we entered.

Inside was a small lobby with some chairs by one wall and a massive tank of water covering the opposite wall. Inside the tank was a computer terminal of some sort and a giant octopus. The cephalopod splayed out several tentacles, changed color multiple times, and let loose a couple jets of water. A speaker on the side of the tank came to life. "So, why do you want to join the guild?"

I moved to the side of the tank closest to the mollusk's large eye. "We're a group of prospectors who just moved here from Ceres. We attempted to sell some tungsten, but the buyer stated that he couldn't take it, because we weren't certified by a guild."

"Naturally. Freelancers are too untrustworthy. How can one be sure that their wares are truly saleable?" A tablet slid out of a slot on the wall opposite of him. "Each of you fill out your personal information. There's a separate file for everyone on that tablet."

Aniya picked up the tablet and filled in her information before handing it to me. It was rather straightforward: "Name: Argentum. Date of birth: 2069. Gender: neuter. E-mail address, voice comm code… " For special skills, I selected both chemical analysis and emergency medic. For employment history, I listed first my work for the corporation that had commissioned my creation, then the Ceres Directorate before the layoffs, and finally my current employment as a freelance prospector. I chose not to fill in any optional references, given our status as fugitives from another asteroid. I then passed the tablet to Cole, who filled it out and passed it to Denal who fitted the device back in its slot.

"All right then. We will need to assess your abilities before accepting your application to join the guild. Tomorrow a representative of the guild will join you on one of your expeditions to observe your techniques and verify your claims." The octopus probably had a script written in his translator specifically for this situation. "Argentum, I am scheduling an examination of your analysis skills in three days time."

Hold on a second there. "But it takes at least two days to reach any asteroids that haven't already been claimed. I'd still be out in space at the time of the exam you have scheduled."

"Chemical analysts do not accompany miners to the dig sites. Guild rules to keep them safe from unnecessary risks. There aren't too many parahumans who know how to identify the minerals we extract properly."

I did not understand. "So miners don't know if they have a load of lanthanides or a chunk of carbon until they get all the way back to port? What if they go broke because they wasted time hauling worthless material when they could have been looking for something more valuable?"

The guild clerk released a bit of ink into the waters of his tank at that statement; I suppose I must have surprised him a bit. "The guild will subsidize your losses. Otherwise, your dues will comprise ten percent of your total profits. The habitat needs carbon too, you know."

"Come on," Aniya grabbed my shoulder in a gesture of reassurance. "We still have enough money left over from the last sale to keep us afloat a little bit longer." She was right; the five hundred thousand qcoins we retained would be enough to finance another expedition, store the tungsten from the last haul in one of the portside warehouses, and pay for our protection plan for another couple weeks.

"Very well," I said with a bit of reluctance. And we left, headed for an increasingly uncertain future.

Chapter 7

The next morning, a grey parrot came to our ship and introduced himself as the observer from the miners' guild, here to evaluate my crewmates for guild membership. While they got to go out rock hunting under scrutiny, I had to stay here on account of "guild regulations". I locked up my lab and emptied my cabin. What I couldn't carry on me was stored in the cargo hold. I would be spending the next four to five days in a moderately priced hotel I had found the night before, while my friends were busy working under the scrutiny of some bureaucrat. And I didn't even have my experiments to keep me from getting bored.

After checking into the hotel I spent the rest of that day reading and looking for bootleg games on the network. The second day, I found some locally produced video drama series about a young Protectors' investigator who seemed to uncover a lot of corpses produced by a variety of psychopaths who killed in distinctive and quite gruesome ways. It managed to hold my interest for a couple hours, impressive for a fifteen minute web show.

Eventually there came the big exam that I had been waiting for, which turned out to be determining the composition of a few vials of iron, platinum, and lead dust. I probably could have told what they were just visually, but I put on a show of using the scales and the spectrophotometer to conduct a detailed and highly specific analysis for the benefit of the bored-looking raccoon assessing me. When it was all over, he printed out a small plastic card declaring me a certified chemical analyst of the dense metal miners' guild and gave it to me for identification.

Feeling like I should at least try to celebrate or something, I went to a somewhat high-priced café for lunch, a place that had tables and parahuman servers rather than just an algae processor and a counter, and ordered a blob of vat-grown beef. I rarely had the chance to eat meat, as even in-vitro animal flesh was expensive several million miles from the nearest pasture, but I felt justified in splurging a little to satisfy my carnivorous instincts that day.

I'd been sawing at the chunk of artificial meat for nearly fifteen minutes when he showed up–a muscular cross-fox wearing synth-leather pants and an open shirt that showed off his pecs. He spotted me and walked over to my table.

"Looks like you're having some trouble there" he stated without so much as a word of introduction.

"I'm used to algae products," I replied as I tore off a chunk of meat and popped it in my mouth. I chewed the tough material vigorously for several seconds before swallowing. Who was this guy to suggest that a canine did not know how to eat meat?

"You should eat meat more often. It's what our ancestors evolved for." True, though he probably meant the foxes that contributed maybe two percent of our DNA rather than the humans who lost their leaf-processing intestines sucking the marrow from gazelle bones. "My name's Walker. What about you, babe?"

Babe? I choked down the last of my mouthful and glared at him. "Argen, and for your information, I'm neither a girl nor an effeminate boy." Most female parahumans have human-like mammary glands, probably added in there by a lonely genetic engineer, so I'm not often mistaken for female.

"Oh, really, now? I like a challenge sometimes." He reached his hand towards mine. About that time, I realized that he didn't really smell right. The genetic engineers deliberately chose not to introduce the genes for the distinctive musk my four-legged kin produced, but my sense of smell was almost as good as theirs, and even without specialized glands there was a subtle difference between each species' scents. That said, I'm not entirely sure whether I realized that Walker smelled more dog-like than foxy before or after I felt the band snap around my wrist.

Surprised, I yanked my arm back. I saw a smart-handcuff, apparently set to close around the first wrist it came across, connected by a thin cable to Walker's arm. There was no apparent matching cuff on his wrist, as if the cable came straight out of his fur. He pulled my arm back down to the table and flipped his own arm to pin it down. He gave me a wicked looking grin as he told me, "Argentum, chemical analyst on Ceres deep space mining vessel ANQ18K458, you are under arrest for the murder of Kurt, clone of Vice President Cooper."

I panicked. With my left hand, I drew my spring knife and slammed it, concealed in my fist, on Walker's arm. Unfortunately, the trick I'd imagined where I would pop the blade into my attacker's flesh didn't work as well as I'd hoped. The blade hit something seemingly impenetrable and the spring sent my arm flying back off his. As I swung back for another hit, he caught my blade arm and forced the knife out of my hand. I reached for my gun, but the seat cushions blocked me from drawing it from my hip holster. He flung me to the ground and attempted to wrestle me into submission. As I struggled, I heard a loud whirring sound, and a quadrotor drone with a pair of automatic gauss rifles on its undercarriage descended upon the open café. The few customers that had stayed behind to gawk hurriedly ran or bounded away. A loud voice erupted from the drone's speakers: "Unidentified parahuman! You will cease assaulting this paying customer of the Marquez Guild and explain yourself!"

Walker scowled at the drone, then hit a space on his right breast before returning his arm to pinning me down. The image of the suggestively dressed cross-fox disappeared, revealing a bloodhound wearing an armored bodysuit. What looked like spider silk with plates of thick composite or metal was strategically spaced all over the suit. I spotted a nick over one of the plates on his cuffed arm where my knife had tried to penetrate.

"I'm Walker, a bounty hunter for the Ceres Directorate. zie has committed a crime against the executives of the Directorate, and I am here to bring zir to justice."

"He was launching missiles at us!" I objected loudly. But before I could say anything further Walker covered my mouth with my own arm.

The drone spoke again. "You will allow zir to stand up and this drone will accompany you two to the nearest Marquez guard station." A pair of red lights on the barrels of each coilgun lit up, presumably the capacitors to the electromagnets. "You have five seconds to comply."

Grudgingly, Walker did comply, yanking me up as he stood so that I stumbled onto my feet. He dragged me along as the drone led us, flying backwards to keep its guns on us, to the station. There we were passed on to a group of mostly feline parahumans in riot gear with large gauss pistols slung on their hips next to a shock baton and a pair of smart-cuffs similar to the ones binding me to the bounty hunter.

We were taken before a massive jaguar whose name tag read "Marquez, Derrick." Was this one of the Guildmaster's clones that Olga Wolf had mentioned? He glowered at us before demanding, "Now what is this all about?"

Walker was the first to speak. "Twenty-six days ago, a freighter piloted by a parahuman known as Kurt went dark near Ceres. Three days later, his ship was found floating derelict; the cockpit was shattered and the body of the pilot was in several hundred frozen pieces. There was just barely enough intact genetic material in a severed hand still attached to the steering column to identify the remains as belonging to Kurt." I could feel myself cringing a bit at the description of the carnage. "The Directorate decided to investigate all ships that had been in the area of the incident at roughly the same time. The only ship that was unavailable for inspection was the one that zir Argentum here was serving aboard. When the Directorate received a request for references from one of the mining organizations here concerning Argentum and zir companions Denal, Aniya, and Cole, we surmised that they were somehow responsible and a bounty was posted."

Derrick glanced first at myself, then at Walker, then

back at me. "When the drone intervened you said something about him 'launching missiles at you.' Would you care to elaborate?"

I suppose I'd already blown my chance to insist that I knew nothing of Kurt's death. I took a deep breath and started to explain. "Twenty-five days ago, we were headed back for Ceres after discovering a significant quantity of gold in one of the lesser asteroids. All of a sudden, our aft sensor pod suffered damage inflicted by a military-grade laser beam. Our pilot, Cole, took us behind another asteroid, and we attempted to hide there. That was when the missiles came. Our automated defense turrets detonated the missiles at a safe distance. A few minutes later, a ship came around as well. We played dead for a while until the other ship came closer and began to extend docking claws." I began to dip my head in regret then. "I panicked and assumed manual control of one of our gauss turrets. I fired a stream of slugs across the ship, and some of them penetrated the cockpit. I did a spectroscopic analysis of the debris and found that some of it was organic in nature."

"This is ridiculous!" Walker objected. "Is zie trying to claim that Kurt was a pirate of some kind after zir gold? He was the clone of a high-ranking executive of the Directorate! Why would he resort to stealing? For all we know, he mined those shiny yellow rocks and zie and zir friends killed him for them!"

"These are both serious accusations the two of you are making," Derrick stated flatly. "Do either of you have video recordings of the event in question?"

"Yes!" Finally, something I could use to defend myself. " I have a copy of the video and the sensor logs on my tablet. It's in my hotel room. I can give you the address and keycard now."

"Now wait a second!" Walker had yet another objection. "Those can be faked."

"My technical team has a lot of experience with falsified evidence," said Derrick. "They'll be able to tell." He motioned for two of his subordinates to take the keycard I had drawn from my kilt pocket and go to the hotel room I mentioned. Then he stared at me. "Piracy is a pretty serious offense pretty much everywhere in the Belt, last I recall. Tell me: Why didn't you think of reporting the incident to the authorities on Ceres?"

"The Directorate does not recognize self-defense as a valid excuse for violence," I explained. "In any case, we found out later that he was the clone of a vice president, so we figured we were better off taking our chances out here."

"Yes, I know how the progeny of the rich and powerful are prone to act." Derrick shot me a grin that looked disturbingly wolfish for a big cat. "Always thinking that they can get away with anything just because they have an influential relative."

Ten minutes later, my tablet was brought in and the video logs of the event were reviewed behind closed doors in a side room. Fifteen minutes after that, the door opened and an officer came back out. Apparently they had found no evidence of editing; the footage was raw from the sensors as far as they could tell.

Derrick called up a still image from the video on his desktop holopad. It displayed the ship that had attacked us. "Is this the victim's spacecraft?" he asked Walker.

"Yes, it is," Walker replied.

The apparent leader of the local guild branch advanced the video several frames until the craft had rotated so that the underside, with the missile tubes, was facing the camera. "Looks a bit heavily armed for a freight craft, especially one that makes berth at a habitat that I just confirmed does not allow violence in self-defense." The bounty hunter started to form a response, but Derrick continued. "I mean, the lasers might be justified as anti-meteor point defense, but the missiles are a bit much, don't you think?"

Walker seemed to be gasping for words at this point, but none came. He slumped forward in defeat. "All right, all right, I'll leave Argentum and zir friends alone."

Derick dismissed the image and began entering something that we couldn't see. "Bounty hunter Walker, you are barred from entering the area of service covered by Guild Marquez. We will also be posting to the board from which you retrieved our client's information, stating that as long as zie is a paying customer of ours, bounty hunters will not be allowed to pursue zir. The video will be mailed to every employee and executive of the Ceres Directorate with a publicly known address." The cuff around my wrist was uncoupled, and Walker was taken out of the room by a pair of officers.

"Thank you," I said. "I was a bit worried there." But as I got up and turned to leave, I felt a strong paw grab onto my tail and pull me back. I looked back and saw Derrick Marquez reaching across his desk to grab me.

"Where do you think you're going? We're not done here yet." I pulled my tail back and sat down again. "You see, when you and your buddies signed on with us, we figured that you were running from conviction for some petty theft or tax evasion or something like that and adjusted your rates accordingly." He sat back down and leaned back with another wolfish grin on his face. "Killing an executive's relative is a much more serious offense, you see. We thus incur many more expenses protecting you from bounty hunters and assassins. I'd say that we'd be justified in doubling, or even tripling, your premiums."

Three thousand qcoins a day, combined with the miners' guild dues and mortgage payments? I didn't want repo men coming after us, too. Not every expedition was as fruitful as the last couple we'd embarked upon. We'd likely go bankrupt within a month or two. "But you're solving that problem for good, aren't you? With the posting and the videos?"

He laughed disturbingly loudly at that statement. "I could count on one hand the number of refugees we cover who had their bounties removed by having evidence of their innocence posted by a bunch of anarchist barbarians." He held up three fingers to show what he meant. "Now, V.P. Cooper might take some flack on the local Ceres blogs for making a pirate. Maybe he'll even lose his job. But in our experience, that only means he'll resort to less-than-legal means of getting his revenge. The next parahumans to come after you might not bother trying to take you alive."

I shuddered. The thought of some camo-suited killer planting a blade in my heart or poisoning my nutrients was not a pleasant one. I supposed I could see his reasoning, but three times our current rate still seemed a bit excessive. I told him that the most we could afford was double our current payments.

"Well, then, maybe this will convince you to reconsider a bit." He called up another video from the logs backed up on my tablet. This one showed the incident as we were arriving on the bridge at the start of the battle–the one where Denal yanked me out of Aniya's slimed pouch-from an angle that quite clearly showed her more private parts. "I don't know about Ceres, but here there's a significant group of you endophiles. A lot of people think that their neurons are a bit cross-wired and have a tendency to avoid them like the plague, especially those parahumans with pouches, with the exception of a few who make a living prostituting themselves to those freaks, and they're ostracized just as badly by the rest of their kind."

I gripped the arms of my chair like my hands were hydraulic vises. I blurted out, "It's not sexual to us!" Then I amended a bit more calmly, "and I thought parahumans had no taboos."

"Yeah, that would be all nice and utopian, now, wouldn't it?" He switched off the hologram and leaned in closer to me. "If everyone were to know what you two get up to in the bedroom and apparently on the bridge, you would be hard pressed to get a job scrubbing out sewage lines. And your friend–Aniya, is it? Well, she would probably end up having twenty of your filthy sewage scrubber colleagues inside her every night just to pay her protection money to the hookers' guild. She might even be picked up by some of the sex slavers that come through here every now and then."

That did it. I couldn't do mass sanitation work to save my life. And poor Aniya shouldn't have to live that horrible way just because she helped me relax in such a way. "Okay, okay. I'll scrape up three times the fee. Just don't include anything in the video to suggest that I like to sleep in her pouch."

"Smart move, foxy," Derrick Marquez said as he slid over a tablet with a form for the new amount for me to sign. "And don't even think of telling anyone that I blackmailed you. I, too, know the advantages of having powerful relatives." He waved to a printed-out photo on the wall behind him, which showed nine nearly identical jaguars, with only their clothes to differentiate them. In the center of the field of view sat a jaguar wearing a closely tailored suit, a scar running down his left cheek marring his features.

Nervously, I quickly applied my thumbprint to the document and left.

When my crew mates arrived the next day, I came back on board the ship and practically leaped into Aniya's arms. "What happened?" she asked, concern clearly showing in her voice.

"I don't want to talk about it." I replied. "Maybe tomorrow, but for now I just want to feel safe." At that she waved off the others and carried me back to her room. There she carefully opened the back of her pants and exposed her hind legs for my access. Grateful for her understanding, and remembering that there weren't any security cameras this far into the ship, I slipped into her pouch and stayed there the whole night.

Chapter 8

A bounty hunter, seriously?" Denal sounded incredulous. "How did he even know we were here?"

It was the day after my friends had come back from their assessment trip. They'd found a decent sized chunk of something dense and grey. They hadn't checked what it was officially, but the readings I'd seen suggested something in the area of osmium. And they had become certified members of the miners' guild like myself, except that they would still be going on these expeditions.

"He said that he tracked us thanks to the miners' guild sending messages asking for references to the Ceres Directorate," I replied. Denal looked a bit guilty about something after my statement. "Anyways," I added, "even if none of us were stupid enough to list some references on their applications, there are several financial records that would place us here: the large-scale exchange of our Ceres qcoins for Vesta's, the mortgage payments we send their way to fend off repossession, et cetera. Probably why he was in the region in the first place; no way he could have flown all the way here from Ceres in the three days since we applied to the guild."

"Not necessarily," Cole threw in. "Vesta is passing fairly close to Ceres now, and there are a lot of ships faster than ours. I'd guess that a bounty hunter would use a fast courier-class ship or maybe a military surplus interceptor if they're chasing people. And maybe we should keep running, to make it harder to find us."

"Cole, with the communication relays connecting every station in the Belt, anywhere we tried to hide would be known everywhere within hours." I found it a bit hard to believe that he was still determined to leave this place. "And most governments would have just let him take me, and you too once you'd come into port. The Marquez Guild reviewed the evidence and sent him packing, even if they tripled our rates."

"Tripled?!" Aniya exclaimed in disbelief. "Can we even afford that?"

"I don't know. Maybe. It depends on how much we can make off these jobs."

"We should move to the Wolf Guild's territory," Denal suggested. I suspected he was still a bit infatuated with that rules-bending investigator who had saved our lives on our first day in the asteroid. "I bet Olga would give us a better price than these guys."

Yep, definitely infatuated. At least he was leaving me alone now.

"Odds are her progenitor would charge us just as much. And that would make the commute to and from the spaceport a regular gauntlet, where anyone who wanted to claim our bounty could go after us. Marquez at least will be able to keep us safe from bounty hunters and hit men near where we live and work." I opted not to mention the real reason, the blackmail.

"So, what are we going to do if we can't afford it?" Cole asked, with a bit of justification, but I thought he still sounded overly critical of Vesta's society.

I came up with an idea that I thought might work. "Our schedule has changed now." I suggested, "I don't go out with you three anymore; instead, I spend almost all my time here on Vesta. Maybe I could do some more analysis work for the guild while you're out mining or something." Surely the miners' guild needed all the analysts they could get if we weren't even allowed in the field.

A week later, I found myself in the minute apartment I'd rented, looking over job listings. It turned out that being the newest chemist in the miners' guild, despite having just as much experience as most of the "senior" members, meant that hardly any jobs were ever thrown your way. I wasn't even allowed to perform the tests on the osmium sample that my friends had brought back. That load, combined with the tungsten we had brought in on the previous run, had barely netted enough to pay the Marquez clan for another couple weeks, what with the guild's ten percent and the storage fees for the tungsten and other assorted expenses. So they were already out on another expedition to find more heavy metals for the guild to profit off.

Did I say "clan" when referring to the Marquez Protectors' Guild? Well, around that time I started to see the Protectors' Guilds for what they truly were. To be honest, I should credit a web show that I started watching while waiting for the miners' guild to send me some work. "Crowns of Furtopia", I think it was. It was this fantasy series that took place on an alternate earth inhabited by parahumans instead of humans and technologically equivalent to tenth-century Europe. The main plotline seemed to involve these families (yes they could reproduce sexually in the fictional world of Furtopia) known alternately as "clans" or "houses" that governed various regions of the country on which the show was set. Apparently, the show had gained such a following on Vesta that some of the terminology had seeped out, and it wasn't uncommon to refer to the Protectors' Guilds as "House Wolf", or "Clan Marquez", or any of a dozen different variations on those, because the leaders of the Guilds had such large clone families. Anyways, it was an impressive piece of work. They filmed with live actors wearing replica Middle Ages clothing on board one of the few bubble-type habitats ever constructed that was pretty heavily terraformed, and they edited out the sloped ground and sky to make it look like it was actually on a planet.

Speaking of those clone families, I had been scrolling through the list of jobs that were currently open on the asteroid when I came across a listing from the Society for the Preservation of Parahuman Species. Curious, I opened the entry and found that it was for a position as a biotechnician in their cloning facility. The pay was substantial, with negotiable hours, but what really caught my attention was the line that stated, "All insurances, health, property, and Protectors' Guild covered entirely." If that meant what I thought it meant, the job was as good as 99% pure platinum for someone like me. I might even make enough to pay for my friends' insurance. I applied immediately.

I was taken by surprise an hour later when I received a call from the SPPS on my tablet. They wanted an interview by video chat already. I opened the chat app and was greeted by the image of a large brown creature that looked halfway between a badger and a bear–a wolverine, I would later learn. I could barely see more than his head but he seemed to be wearing some sort of white lab coat or possibly a ceremonial robe of some kind with intricate designs of DNA helixes patterned up and down the lapels in gold. The interviewer directed his large brown eyes at mine and introduced himself. "Good morning Argentum. My name is Caleb Burns, and I'm here to determine if you're the type of parahuman the Society for the Preservation of Parahuman Species needs in order to continue our most worthy goal of ensuring the survival of our culture."

That was an interesting question. "The type of parahuman the SPPS needs?" What types of parahumans was he referring to? Species of non-human genes? Skill sets? Body type? I couldn't tell what he was referring to, so I started to talk about my hobbies: "Well, I have been performing my own DNA tests using the genetic material of myself and my crewmates for about four years, attempting to find the genes that were modified to make me a neuter instead of male or female."

This Caleb being was obviously not too interested in my statement, probably because I had already listed my hobby of messing with the codes of life. "Yes, yes, but what exactly was it that persuaded you to apply for this position?"

I thought that saying "the insurance coverage" wouldn't be particularly well received, so I chose to share the other thing that had attracted me to the opening. "That advertisement, with the human picking over the remains of parahuman civilization after we've all died off. I thought it was rather inspiring."

He stared at me with an expression of surprise on his face. "Really? Those ads worked? I thought they would never convince anyone. You know, the idea of family being too foreign for most parahumans."

Family? Oh, the last scene with the clone taking care of his ailing progenitor. "I suppose some things are just embedded in our genes."

"Yes, yes, I suppose they are. The directive to propagate those genes being one of the strongest, I suppose. Would explain why the Guildmasters all rushed to support the old man when he offered them additional clones." The wolverine suddenly seemed to realize that he'd said something he hadn't intended to let slip and covered his mouth with two pairs of hands, or rather one pair of hands and one pair of paws—it seemed he was a taur. Slowly, he moved his hands and paws away and continued. "Anyhow, speaking of clones, what do you think of them?"

I thought back to the vice president's clone who attempted to kill us and the Marquez clone that threatened to expose certain details of my and Aniya's lives. One's progenitors had sought disproportionate retribution for his death and the other's had apparently enabled him to extort extra money from their customer base. But I also recalled the message presented by that ad, as well as Denal's half-serious comment about our group getting a bunch of clones once we had enough to commission them all. I thought of the possibility of those powerful people's clones becoming the entirety of parahumanity within the next century. They might even become the majority within my own lifespan and make my last few years a living hell before I broke down and ceased to be. "I believe that we need to think about our future. And clones are the future for our kind."

"That's good to hear," Caleb replied. "It says here that you came to Vesta recently aboard a mining ship originally from Ceres. And you're a registered member of the Dense Metals Miners' Guild here. Why would you want to join the SPPS when you're already employed?"

Not good. I couldn't tell him why I needed more money. That would be the interview equivalent of suicide. "They don't give very many jobs to new chemical analysts. They didn't even allow me to do the purity control for my former crew's hauls." I contemplated whether I should tell him a bit about the high insurance rates I'd been subjected to.

"And I'll bet that the Marquez Guild has been extorting a lot of qcoin from you since you just showed up on Vesta, haven't they?"

I was instantly horrified at that statement. How much did he know? "Maybe, a little." I tried to sound calm but was finding it difficult.

"Well, don't worry about that." Caleb Burns shot me a wink and smiled. "Jakob Griggs and Jerome Marquez are old buddies. I'm sure if you sign on, he'll figure out a way to cut your rates down a bit."

Cut my rates? How much influence did the SPPS have? "I was under the impression that all insurances would be covered."

"Well…" Caleb shrugged and slicked back the fur on his head. I could guess that I had caught him in something. "Technically, it's deducted from your paycheck, but we can usually convince them to lower their rates significantly, and the pay we offer is considerable in and of itself."

"How much is 'considerable'?" I found myself asking.

He quoted me a rather respectable pay rate, though not quite enough for me to live on with the increased Marquez fees. But if he was telling the truth about the Society's leader having the ability to lower the insurance paid by his employees, I might even be able to help cover my crewmates as well. I agreed to come over to their facilities for an in-person interview and tour. At the very least I could get a look at their labs for myself.

The SPPS's headquarters was a five-story building built into the cave wall of the cavern covered by the Marquez Guild. The front face of the structure was halfway covered with animated holograms similar to the one I had seen earlier, along with murals of DNA helixes and parahumans in biofabrication tanks and other stuff like that. I walked up to the front doors made of stained glass that showed a nude male savannah cat with his arms and legs spread out in a pattern that made it look like he had four arms and four legs. Wonder what that was supposed to mean?

Caleb Burns was standing by the front counter in the main lobby. My guess that he was a taur was correct, and he had somehow managed to tie his robe-slash-lab coat in such a way that it enclosed his hind legs without showing anything. He saw me and gave a slight bow in my direction. I returned the gesture.

"Hello, Argentum. Welcome to our humble cloning laboratory for the preservation of the parahuman clade. Are you ready to begin the tour?"

I assented, and the wolverine turned to a sealed hatch next to the counter, marked "Decontamination Chamber." He swung it open and gestured for me to follow. We found ourselves in a room filled with light environment suits hung on racks in a variety of shapes and sizes. Caleb removed his robe and wriggled into a large taur-shaped suit. I did the same with my kilt and vest and a medium-sized bipedal suit with enough tail space.

"Through this door is our main production floor," he explained, speaking through an external speaker on the front of his suit. "We have a lot of delicate equipment and biological substances out there. The last thing we need is contamination from loose fur or someone breathing too hard."

I supposed I could understand that, though I had to wonder about the state of my own experiments, seeing how I hadn't bothered with airtight seals on my safety equipment. "Will this be where I will be working?" I asked him.

"Part of the time. You'll probably be in quality control, making sure there's no unforeseen mutations in the cell cultures." He was speaking fairly quickly. "Most of your work will be done in the side labs."

He opened the other door and we walked out into a massive room that probably qualified as a cavern. There were at least three stories' worth of machinery, all chugging along and mixing some vat of cells or pumping some fluid into a tank like the one the clone at the end of the ad emerged from. One of the tanks had a bluish skeleton inside, which brought to mind the long-decayed corpse in the same ad, while another adjacent tank had a body that was almost complete, half-covered in a layer of skin.

"You'll mostly be coming out here to take samples from the cell cultures." He pointed at a set of small vats hanging suspended above one of the biofabrication tanks. "It's almost completely automated. All we need to keep this running are a couple of technicians who perform maintenance and repairs every few weeks."

We came to a stairway leading upwards to a large room

with a glass wall facing the production floor. I could see a half-dozen parahumans of various species in hazmat suits fussing over a variety of beakers, test tubes, petri dishes, and gene sequencers similar to the ones I had on our ship but obviously much more expensive. As we entered, a tall male who appeared to be a spotted cat of some sort, possibly a savannah cat like the one on the front door, approached us.

"This is Maximus Griggs, supervisor of this team." Caleb said. "Maximus, this is Argentum. Zie is interested in the open position here."

"Good to see you, Silver." He gave me a rather cat-like smile as he said this. I guessed that he knew enough ancient Latin to know what my name meant. "You have any prior experience with genetic testing and mutation screening?"

"I've performed some experiments on my own," I began to tell him, "trying to engineer nutrient algae that tasted like bacon. And performing DNA tests on myself to figure out why the parts shops can't make me a set of sexual organs."

"You're neuter then?" Max inquired quizzically. Not that I blamed him; even without this baggy suit, it was hard to tell my actual gender or lack thereof. I nodded. "Well, we do some organ replacement and augmentation on the side." My ears perked up, which I'm sure was noticeable even under that suit of mine. "We found we can give neuters a cock or a vag, or even both, but unfortunately the gonads require genetic alterations that cause the immune system to reject them without a lot of drugs."

My ears flicked downwards in disappointment. What good would a pole or a hole be without the sex drive to use it? And I was still a bit in denial of the drive I had at that point. "Well, I hope I have the chance to contribute to something a bit more important here."

"You will. We're building the future for all the diverse parahuman species here." He waved back at the production floor we'd just left.

At that moment, something about his name clicked in my head. "Are you by any chance related to Jakob Griggs, the founder of the SPPS?"

Maximus snorted loudly at my inquiry. "Oh, I'm related, all right. I'm one of his clones." I was afraid of that. Would he act like two-thirds of the other clones I'd met? "But Dad wasn't the founder; that was his progenitor, who was simply named Griggs. He died in an accident a year before my brothers and I were decanted."

He was a clone of a clone? "Sounds like he's a bit young to be running something this important."

The second-generation clone smiled at me before speaking further. "Maybe but we learn fast you know. Look at me. I'm barely two years old and already I'm supervising an entire lab."

So the same nepotism I'd seen on Ceres and in the Marquez Guild existed here too. At least the one who would be my boss seemed agreeable enough. And the pay and benefits package were pretty good. "So, where do I sign?"

Chapter 9

I started work the next day. It wasn't particularly difficult work, mind you, but I was being entrusted with the well-being of the future people of Vesta. They started me off with an evaluation by the supervisor of one of the other teams in the department, detecting mutations in previously tested samples. On one occasion, I found a deletion in the thirteenth chromosome that my instructor hadn't found; he claimed that I had made a mistake and started to go over the sequence again, only to notice one of the codons was missing an adenosine. He changed my assessment and mumbled something about how it must have happened after his own analysis.

Regardless, I found myself making almost as much as my share of a decent haul of ore back before we moved to Vesta, and I was forced to go back to my lonely little apartment. The Society made good on their promise to arrange for my Protection rates to be lowered. I still paid more than I had my first couple weeks on the asteroid, but it was now affordable. Unfortunately, there were only a couple hundred qcoins left after expenses to help my friends pay their fees. I sincerely hoped that they found some more valuable minerals like the mascon we had found just before the incident.

My job wasn't simply to detect mutations, it was also to determine whether a mutation was worth fixing. Many mutations—a few extra letters in an intron here, an Alu element deleted there—were harmless and would have no effect on the parahuman being printed out. If something actually changed the phenotype, such as hemophilia, we then had to decide whether it would be more cost-effective to try to correct the defect with gene therapy or throw out that batch and grow another one. Both would add significantly to the customer's final bill for the clone, the relative expense of either option depending largely on what stage the mutation was caught at. Preferably, the mutations were to be caught early on, before too many nutrients had been expended growing defective cells.

We had a database of several common genetic diseases, but sometimes we came across a deviation that we lacked a prior record for. In those cases, we had a simulator.

The simulator had access to several times the total combined processing power of every computer that existed on Planet Earth during the first couple decades of the twenty-first century. Now, of course, every major university on Earth had a far more powerful machine than ours, but it was still greater than most parahumans' entire guild's or corporation's combined computing strength. And our simulator used every microsecond of its immense CPU cycles predicting the results of the completely unheard-of mutations we fed into it.

The results we got out of it were often astonishingly bizarre. One time it predicted that the fur of any parahuman fabricated with the mutation in question would grow in fluorescent green. Another time, it predicted that the cells would undergo apoptosis in three to six hundred generations. We kept a sample from that one to confirm, and the cells did indeed liquefy after approximately four hundred and thirteen divisions.

Then one day, about two months after I had started working full time in the lab and discarded my miners guild membership entirely, I came across a deletion in the promoter region of a certain gene that changed everything.

"PROMOTER TO MOR10X-6 ENCODING GENE DISABLED", the readout from the simulator declared. "PROTEIN MOR10X-6 EXPRESSION MINIMAL TO NON-EXISTENT. POSSIBLE RESUMPTION OF MEIOTIC DIVISION."

Meiosis? As in the form of cellular division whereby cells divide into cells with half the minimum number of chromosomes in preparation for fusion with another cell that lacks a full complement of chromosomes? I opened the genetic database and attempted to look up MOR10X-6. What I got was a message stating, "CLEARANCE REQUIRED. PLEASE INPUT REGISTRATION NUMBER AND PASSWORD."

Confused, I showed it to Maximus. He took one look at it and shrugged. "A lot of our equipment and data comes from loot seized from the biogenesis corporations in the revolution. Occasionally you come across something that they tried to lock up, keep hidden from us peons and slaves."

He then did something completely in violation of safety regulations: He opened his containment suit and started fishing around for something. "Some hackers cracked the codes a while ago and sold them to the SPPS. I've got them written down here somewhere." He pulled out a folded square of flexible plastic. There were apparently a set of numbers and passwords printed on the inside fold of the plastic. He entered three different sets of codes into the tablet before access was granted to the restricted files. When it opened, he held the tablet up to his face, obscuring it from my view. As he read, his expression changed from confusion to surprise, then to something I couldn't quite identify. He passed me the tablet.

I read the proffered entry. It was just as I suspected: MOR10X-6 was an artificial gene constructed by an agronomics corporation in the first quarter of the twenty-first century to protect genetic copyrights. It produced a protein that interfered in the process of meiotic division, making it all but impossible to proceed but allowing the gonads to otherwise function normally, apparently creating a healthy but infertile genetically modified organism that would not go around pirating the company's intellectual property all willy-nilly. In other words, it was the gene that made us reliant on cloning.

"This… is serious," was all I could think to say at that time. It was certainly true, if a bit of an understatement.

"I need to show this to my dad." Max grabbed the tablet back from me and held it tightly to his chest as he ran off to alert his progenitor. I figured there was nothing else to do now but wait so I just picked out another tablet and returned to my work.

Approximately an hour and a half later, I was called up to Jakob Griggs' office. I handed my current project off to a co-worker and walked to the elevator. The elevator car had seven buttons inside: one for each of the regular floors, one for a sublevel basement cut into the cavern floor, and one that was accessible only by biometric scan or remote operation. Before I could look up which floor the head of the Society's office was on, the elevator started moving upwards. It went past the fifth floor to something marked with a "J" on the electronic readout. As I stood dumbfounded the door opened onto a wide-open space overlooking the city below. It appeared that Jakob Griggs worked on the roof of the building.

In the middle of the expanse, there stood a large table covered with food items that I had only seen in images and video before: stuffed turkeys, carved T-bone steaks, lobster, ham with the bone still inside... How much had that whole thing cost? On a chair at the far side of the table sat a savannah cat, like Maximus, wearing a black robe embroidered with crystals forming the shapes of DNA helixes. He raised his head to glance at me as I slowly, nervously came forward.

"Ahh, Argentum. Good to finally meet you." He spoke to me in the same voice as my supervisor. "Please, get yourself into something more comfortable and join me for lunch."

He gestured to my right, and I followed his hand with my eyes.

I saw a coat rack with a white robe in the same patterns as the one Caleb Burns had been wearing when we first met, though fitted and sized more for a biped of my height and weight. I looked down at my own bulky, uncomfortable containment suit. "Oh, I guess this would be a bit awkward to eat in." But then I noticed a lack of enclosed spaces to change in.

Jakob saw me looking around puzzled and chortled loudly. "Don't worry." He made a show of covering his eyes with the sleeve of his own robe. "I won't look."

I supposed I could see where Maximus got his humor

from. I unzipped myself from my hazmat suit as quickly as possible and threw the robe on. Hopefully he wouldn't mind my getting sweat all over it. It was surprisingly comfortable, as if it were made from soft plant fibers instead of the bacterial plastics we made most of our clothes from in the Belt. It must have been made from materials imported from Earth, like the feast before me.

I stepped awkwardly towards the chair on the opposite end of the table, presumably where I was meant to sit. At the sound of the chair legs scraping along the floor, Mr. Griggs put his arm back down and saw me cautiously sitting down.

"I take it you've never had real meat before, M. Argentum?" he inquired, to which my only answer was a short nod. "Not surprising. It is quite expensive to import anything from Earth or Mars to begin with. Perishable items such as animal flesh even more so." He speared another piece of steak on his fork and raised it to his mouth before speaking again. "Please, try the chicken. It's unlikely you'll get another chance to try it soon."

Knowing he was right, and finding the fragrance too hard to resist, I tore off a leg from the roasted bird in the center of the table. Discovering it difficult to keep my manners, I tore into it with a ferocity I found hidden deep within the few genes I had not inherited from any human. I had eaten vat-grown poultry before, partially to see Cole's reaction to my consuming tissue from his own taxonomic class (not much, it turns out; apparently corvids are as close to fowl as foxes are to cows or something along those lines), but this bore little resemblance. This was juicy, tender, with a crisp skin that the tissue vats seemed to leave out. Within a matter of minutes, I had stripped the leg to the bone.

As I tossed the oddly white and flexible bone aside, Jakob Griggs spoke again. "That was actually the turkey, but whatever you prefer." I made an effort to keep my embarrassment from showing, but apparently he could see it anyways. "Don't worry about it," he said with a wave of his hand. "I'm sure this is the first time you've been able to tell the difference between one meat and another."

But then his expression changed all of a sudden, becoming ice cold as he stared at me from across the table. "So, I hear you found out about one of the corporations' biggest secrets."

I think I felt my fur stand up at that simple statement. Something about the tone those ordinary words were issued in chilled me. "Well," I started, a bit nervous and taken off guard by the sudden shift in his demeanor, "it was completely by accident, but I believe I discovered a mutation that deactivates the gene that renders us, I mean, you and other parahumans with sex organs, infertile." I had to correct myself, as there was definitely more than one simple gene that prevented neuters like myself from making babies.

"I see." Jakob reached for a small box on the table with a set of holes in the lid. "And just what do you intend to do with that mutation?"

"Me?" I asked incredulously. "Well, I doubt I would do much with it, but I suppose one could use a targeted mutagen to damage the gene and enable their testes or ovaries to undergo spermatogenesis or oogenesis, respectively. Possibly even use a CRISPR interference technique to knock out the entire gene." The equipment to do either was fairly plentiful. It was far safer than gene therapy to simply create a compound that would bond to a specific gene sequence and destroy it in the rare instance of a harmful mutation that involved an addition rather than a deletion or transposition.

"Yes." He then shot me a look that made me shrink back into my seat in primal fear. "And what do you think would happen to the Society for the Preservation of Parahuman Species if parahumans began to use that mutagen you're suggesting and started replicating themselves on their own?"

I paused as I thought about it for a minute. "Most people wouldn't need clones; they'd just find a friend of the opposite gender and produce new parahumans like most natural animals and humans do." I realized at that moment that my job could be at stake. "But there would still be neuters like myself who would still need clones to continue their gene-lines. And some people who simply prefer clones for some reason." I thought of one more thing. "And besides, wouldn't your goal of preserving parahumanity be accomplished?"

Jakob let out a low growl. My ears flattened, and I felt my head slipping down beneath my robe, attempting to hide from the large and angry predator before me. He addressed me once more. "Our goal doesn't just encompass creating the next generation so that our species can outlive our individual selves. There are other factors that we don't generally discuss with the public."

He shook the box he had picked up a minute earlier, and I could hear a faint squeaking sound from within. "Are you familiar at all with the net series 'Crowns of Furtopia'?" he asked me. I nodded faintly and he continued. "Feudalism is the default state of any large group of animals. Individuals work to preserve their own genelines and band together with their kin to compete with other kin groups. The smart ones get the weaker groups to produce resources for them in exchange for protection from more short-sighted opportunists. Human history has proven time and time again that in the absence of any other form of government, feudalism re-emerges. And I am sure that you are starting to see that to be true here on Vesta as well."

I thought back to the pop culture references to the Protectors' Guilds as clans and houses, how every high-ranking official in the Guilds that I'd met had been clones of the Guild leaders, and what they were getting away with because of their relationship. "But... your progenitor was the one who enabled them to form kinship groups in the first place?" I asked nervously.

"Yes, and that is how I continue to keep them in line." Jakob Griggs made another toothy grin that somehow intimidated me more than his growl had. "If I weren't able to threaten them with the revocation of their access to my cloning tanks, they would be constantly fighting one another over territory like the animals they are. As it is, the balance of power between the Protection Guilds is as unstable as a barrel of nitroglycerin."

I believed that I understood now. "And you think if they were able to perpetuate their genelines on their own they would turn Vesta into a twenty-second century version of Furtopia?"

"I know they will." Jakob opened the box he was holding. He reached inside and withdrew a live mouse. I was amazed. That was the first time I had ever seen a non-sapient animal. My unspoken question of what he intended to do with the mouse was answered when he slung his head back, opened his mouth, and dropped the mouse in. There was a sickening snap and crunch of bones breaking and he swallowed loudly. Licking the remaining blood from his lips he started to explain. "Live mice, expensive even by my standards. Do you want to know why they're so expensive?"

"Because the freighters need extra life support to keep them alive all the way out to the Belt?" I feebly suggested.

"That is the bulk of it, yes." Jakob nodded. "But another expense is the sterilization procedures they have to perform on every one of the mice before they leave earth orbit." I gave a confused expression, prompting him to continue. "If so many as one male and one female mouse are fertile in the same cargo module, they will inevitably find a way to mate and produce dozens of baby mice every few weeks. And each of those babies will be able to make more babies within a month of birth. By the time they get all the way out here, the life support system of their module is overtaxed, and you get a load of decaying mouse carcasses. Do you see my point?"

I was afraid I didn't, but I wasn't sure I wanted to tell that to the very self-assured cat who essentially owned all the law enforcement organizations on the asteroid, so I stayed silent.

Apparently, my silence was answer enough, as he spoke again. "Sapient beings are no different. Humans almost depleted their own ecosystem on Earth; it's the whole reason they sent us out into space to obtain more resources for them to consume. By controlling the price of cloning, we prevent Vesta from becoming overpopulated and overstraining the flimsy life support systems we have in place."

"Surely people are smart enough to stop reproducing before they reach the carrying capacity of their environment," I objected. I could not imagine anyone being so stupid.

"And are you willing to bet the lives of everyone on this asteroid, possibly the entire Belt, on that statement?" I could not. That was too big a decision for me to make. I slumped my head forward and shook it lightly. "So you will not tell anyone else about your discovery?"

"Yes," I told him, defeat plain on my face.

"Excellent," Jakob Griggs said before popping another mouse into his mouth. After swallowing he asked me another question. "Did you tell anyone else before coming here?"

"Just your clone, Maximus."

"Good. I've already told him why he should keep his mouth shut." Jakob looked back into the box of mice one last time and turned back to me. "It appears that I have no more appetite for mice today, but there is still one left here. Would you care to try it?"

At that point, I was afraid to refuse anything he asked of me. I walked up to his side of the table and glanced down at the box. There was one white mouse remaining, among the stains left by its siblings in the container, still trying in vain to scurry up the slick walls of the box. I reached in and tried to grab it but it ran away to try and vault the opposite wall. I reached in with my other hand and herded it between the two. I managed to take hold of its thin tail and pull it out. Screeching in terror, it tried to wriggle out of my hand or curl back on my fingers and claw at them, but to no avail. Looking into its beady black eyes, I steeled myself for what would come next. I opened my mouth and tried to lead the rodent inside. Still clinging to a faint hope of survival, it gripped onto my tongue with its sharp toes. The pain instead prompted me to bite down hard. I heard the ribs crack, felt the squishy organs spill out of the holes in its torso, the hot blood streaming down my chin. Not knowing exactly what to do next, I flicked the corpse to the back of my mouth with my tongue and, with a great deal of effort, swallowed.

"You have a bit of something there." Jakob Griggs, the shadowy director of the anarchy of Vesta, gestured to his left cheek. I picked up a napkin and dabbed it at the approximate area he had indicated. It came back stained dark red. If I had been superstitious, I might have taken it as an omen of things to come.

Chapter 10

A few days after my encounter with my all-powerful employer, I was eating dinner with my former crewmates. Nothing anywhere near the quality of that veritable feast Jakob Griggs had, just some flavored lichen-based foodstuffs that grew in some of the smaller caves set aside for food production. To be honest, I hadn't had much of an appetite after that eventful luncheon. I was cutting up a greenish loaf when Cole spoke.

"It's funny," he said to no one in particular. "Just a couple days ago, all our rates went up ten percent. Wonder what changed this time?"

"No idea," I said. I really did have no idea what he was talking about. My own rates hadn't changed since I started working for the SPPS. Why would everyone else's rise?

Denal offered his own thoughts. "Well, I asked some of the boys and girls I know by the docks. They said that Marquez hadn't upped their own bills by any significant amount."

"So it's just us?" said Aniya, who was tearing off chunks of two whole loaves of lichen bread as we talked. "You think it's because of the whole bounty hunter thing?"

"Doubt it; it's been weeks," Cole said. "Unless

something else happened with Argen over in the genetics labs."

I paused for a second. I couldn't tell them anything about MOR10X-6; I had promised Jakob I wouldn't tell anyone. "No, nothing like that." Which was true in the vaguest sense. I had not encountered any bounty hunters or anything like that.

"Here's an idea," Denal began, which probably meant it was doomed to fail. "That Derrick Marquez guy is just a big bully, like that VP's kid we splattered out by Ceres. He's not used to people standing up to him, so how about we miss a payment or two, and when he comes over looking for money, we firmly, and with our weapons well at hand, tell him we're not paying the increased rate?"

I could tell from the start that it was a bad idea. "Look," I told him, "I still have some money left over after the insurance deductions. I could give it all to you guys and just live off the algal dole."

"And what about when the premiums get too high for even that to help?" Aniya asked.

I honestly hadn't thought of that possibility, though I doubted my income could make much of a difference as it was. "Look," I said, "you do not want to fight this guy. You just don't."

"Maybe you don't, Argen, but the rest of us do." Even Cole was in on this idiotic plan. What was going on here? "You don't have to participate but we are going to convince him to stop charging us such exorbitant prices, one way or another."

"Fine then!" I threw down my utensils and got up to storm out. "Just don't come running to me when you need to pay your medical bills after this fiasco goes down."

The next day, I headed down to the ship after work, thinking that maybe I'd reacted a bit too harshly to their plan and should have offered some more coherent arguments as to why it would be a bad idea to try to intimidate Derrick Marquez into lowering our payments. All day I had been thinking of new arguments that I hoped would persuade them more effectively. But all those ideas were dashed from my mind as I came around the bend and saw Marquez enforcers setting up a perimeter of yellow tape around the docking tunnel to our vessel.

"What's going on here?" I asked the nearest officer, an almost two-meter-tall tiger.

His response was to hold a camera up to my face and run my image through a tablet app. When he read the results, he glared down at me and instead of answering my question, issued a question (or rather a demand) of his own. "Where is the red panda known as 'Denal'?"

What? They wanted Denal? Had he tried something stupid already? The only response I could think to give was a short "I... don't know."

"You liar." The tiger grabbed the front of my shirt and drew me close. "You two were on the same policy as the victims; you must have some idea of where he ran off to."

"Leave zir." A disturbingly familiar voice came from a gurney set up by the Guild vehicle parked next to the tunnel entrance. On the propped up stretcher was the one cat I least wanted to see at that time. "Zie's with Griggs," said Derrick Marquez, the corrupt clone of the Marquez clan's leader.

The enforcer dropped me and stalked off, back to whatever it was he had been assigned to do. Cautiously, I approached the commander. I saw that his stomach was bandaged and he was essentially confined to his impromptu bed by a set of intravenous tubes and straps to his legs.

"What..." I stuttered, afraid of what the answer might be. "What was he talking about?"

Derrick snorted; even such a simple act appeared to take a great deal of effort in his condition. "What do you think happened?" He lifted a hand to point towards the interior of the ground car next to him. "Your raccoon buddy went nuts and shot your other two friends. Then when I tried to stop him, he attempted to run me through with a sword."

I looked in the direction he was pointing. There, sitting on the bed of the transport lay several items in plastic bags tagged with numbers for reference. One bag had Denal's longsword, the thin blade snapped in half. Aniya and Cole's dart guns were in another pair of bags, next to them a couple of darts that had apparently been fired. But the interior of the vehicle was dominated by a pair of very large opaque bags that were zipped shut. One was just a little over one meter long, the other well over three.

"Are they..." I started to ask, but I couldn't bring myself to complete the sentence. "They can't be. I was just having dinner with them last night. It's not possible."

"Afraid so, Silver." The Marquez scion's voice was calm and controlled, as if this kind of thing were routine. "The darts Denal shot them with where loaded with massive doses of hydrogen cyanide. They were dead within minutes."

"But those are Aniya and Cole's guns," I objected, still unable to grasp the reality laid out before me. "They would never put something so lethal in their darts; they hated killing."

"Then I guess you didn't know your crewmates as well as you thought you did." Derrick Marquez started to lift himself up off his stretcher to turn towards me. "I suggest you go home and go to bed early. This is a lot to deal with." Then his eyes lit up in a moment of sadistic glee. "Unless… this was your home, wasn't it? Well, too bad, because it's now evidence in a murder investigation. You might be able to retrieve some of your things in two to six weeks, depending on how long the paperwork takes to process."

"Hope you can handle the mortgage payments," I said in a weak attempt at a witty comeback as I slowly walked away in the direction of the apartment I had called home for five nights out of each of the last five weeks.

Once I made it there, I found myself taking Derrick Marquez's advice, piling every blanket and pillow in the apartment on top of the bed and burrowing underneath them. It was no substitute for Aniya's pouch. That would never again offer me the comfortable safety I had felt inside it. By the time I crawled out to inform Maximus that I wouldn't be coming in to work the following morning, the sheets were stained with sweat and tears.

I spent the day following the deaths of two of my closest and only friends and the disappearance of the third sitting in my bedroom wrapped in a blanket and watching video streams. Having fully realized that I was living in a feudal nightmare, I lost my taste for "Crowns of Furtopia" and began watching comedy shows. There were hundreds of antique human comedies on the net (watching our great creators whacking each other on the heads with hammers never got old) as well as original parahuman works, often commenting on current events in one asteroid or another. But then one of the not-so-serious news feeds I was watching led me to one that was serious, and a bit personal.

This was a video titled "Newcomer to Vesta Stabs Marquez Clone, why?" and was uploaded by someone who went by the moniker of "HoundOfGod." The last thing I needed was a reminder of what had just happened, but curiosity led me onwards.

The video started with a still image of Derrick Marquez staggering with a bloody, broken blade sticking out of his kevlar body armor, the hilt of Denal's sword in his hand and an expression of pure fury on his face. The voiceover began in digitally distorted harsh and gravelly tones; it sounded male, but for all I knew, the narrator was actually female or neuter and using software to hide their identity. "Yesterday, Derrick Marquez, a commander in the Marquez Protectors Guild, was stabbed by an individual known simply as Denal." The image changed to a street camera view of Denal from one of our first days in Vesta. "Denal arrived on Vesta over a month ago with three companions: Aniya" -a picture of Aniya in her spacesuit was shown–"Cole"–the raven's portrait–"and Argentum," -me, obviously. "The four of them had slain a pirate in self-defense near Ceres a couple weeks prior to their arrival at Vesta, who just happened to be a clone of a prominent VP in the Directorate hierarchy. How ironic that they chose Vesta to escape reprisal for slaying a clone." If only we'd known, Aniya and Cole might have been doing hard labor instead of lying in some morgue waiting to be recycled into raw nutrients. "The official report by House Marquez is that during negotiations with the commander over insurance premiums, Denal suddenly slew Aniya and Cole with pressure darts loaded with cyanide, then charged Derrick with a Jiàn sword. The blade then broke in his attempt to penetrate the commander's bodysuit, and Denal fled." I did not need to be reminded; as the video stated this I pulled the sheets closer together over my eyes.

"However, there is one major problem with this account. After fleeing the scene Denal ran straight to territory covered by House Wolf and pled for asylum. What's more, he had a video recording of the encounter taken via a mini-camera in one of his vest buttons." So that answered where Denal was, hiding behind his lupine girlfriend's camouflage and gun. "The following video has been determined to be the original footage with no editing, for the simple reason that he had no time to edit while running for his life."

The video suddenly shifted to a scene of Derrick Marquez sitting at the far end of a table from the camera. To either side of the camera, one could barely see some black feathered wings and furred paws resting on the table. "Now," said Derrick, "I'm sure you can understand why we had to increase your rates so drastically, considering your present safety concerns."

"Yeah, right." The person wearing the camera had spoken, given how the image jostled, and I instantly recognized the voice as Denal's. "You just want to suck every spare qcoin we own out of us."

"There are additional expenses racked up by fending off bounty hunters after your hide," Derrick continued. "And your foxy friend is no longer paying zir share of the extra costs, so you three have to take up the slack."

"What?" The camera view shifted to the left, just barely showing Aniya expressing disbelief at this statement. "Argen's not paying?"

"We have a bit of an agreement with zir employers." The camera shifted back to Derrick.

"That does not mean that we have to pay for zir." It shifted to the right this time, showing Cole gripping the table tightly in all four sets of talons.

"I say it does." Derrick stood up and popped the strap holding his sidearm in place.

"He's going to shoot! Get him!" It was hard to tell, but it looked like Denal was scrambling across the table, sword drawn, and pouncing on Derrick. It was moving fast, but I could just barely make out several sounds of darts flying before the jaguar was thrown down to the ground with the sword embedded in his bodysuit.

"Argh, you idiot." Derrick shoved Denal loudly off himself. There was a snap of metal breaking as he did so. When Denal landed, he saw Aniya and Cole lying prone on the floor, their bodies twitching and their mouths filling with foam. There was a sharp intake of breath as Denal noted the darts in their necks, the glazed lifeless look on their faces. Then he ran, deeper into the bowels of the ship, no doubt hoping that he could lose the presumably relentless pursuer just standing up behind him.

I stopped the video at that point. First Denal was not only a lecher but a murderer; then he was an innocent framed for the deaths of our closest friends by a corrupt Guildmaster's progeny? What was truth and what were lies? How could I decide?

Chapter 11

I tried to return to life as usual in the lab the next day, but my mind kept wandering back to Aniya and Cole. I mixed a couple of reactions improperly, and the resulting readings were impossible to decipher, wasting hours of effort. After the third ruined experiment, Maximus spoke to me.

"Are you all right?" he asked, knowing full well that I was not all right but still asking to be polite regardless.

"No," I told him, not wanting to elaborate further.

"I heard about your friends."

At that comment, I ripped off my headgear and snarled at him. "What did you hear?!"

"Well," Maximus started, "I heard two different accounts: one stating that one of the parahumans you came to Vesta with shot your other two companions and stabbed a Marquez." I think I felt my claws start to penetrate my glove as I clenched my fist in fury. "And the other stating that Marquez shot two of your friends and the third one stabbed him in retaliation." I relaxed slightly at this statement; he'd apparently seen more than one version of the night's events. "Do you know what really happened?" he asked.

I shook my head. "The second version sounds more

like what I know of Denal, but who knows what happened?" I wasn't too sure I wanted to tell him about the plan to violently persuade Derrick Marquez to lower our coverage rates.

Maximus glanced at the piece of my environment suit that was in my hands instead of covering my head, then back at my face. "Maybe we shouldn't talk in here, if you insist on not wearing that while we're doing so." He gestured to a door leading to a maintenance corridor meant for the custodians. I found myself following him out.

Once we were outside the lab, Maximus started to get out of his hazard suit as well. I could see that he, too, had a preference for "going commando." The corridor was dark, with only a string of small lights along the ceiling to light up the bare stone walls. He shoved his suit in a pocket in the wall opposite the door and indicated that I should do the same.

"Uh, why?"

"It gets hot in here. Even less ventilation than in the lab." That made sense. Only with the fans were the suits bearable at all. I threw off my suit, figuring that I had even less to hide than he did, and if he was flaunting it like that, I could too. Max picked up my discarded containment suit, folded it up, and put it in the same cavity as his own suit. Then he shoved a rock over the hole and covered our suits completely. He turned to me abruptly. "Okay, that should cover up the audio sensors in our suits. So what didn't you want to tell me before?"

I was more than a bit surprised there, I hadn't known that there were audio sensors in the clothes. I had expected that Maximus would simply tell his progenitor anything I told him. "Why would you do that?" I asked. "I assume it would be more convenient for your father to simply listen in on our conversation rather than wait for you to repeat it to him."

He looked at me aghast. "Not everything I do is for my progenitor. I have a life apart from him, you know." Maximus sat down on the stony floor and gestured for me to join him, which I did. "I've actually been finding reasons to disagree with him. I don't think that Jakob Griggs really has the best interest of parahumanity in mind."

This intrigued me. "What do you mean?"

"I mean that his efforts to 'preserve' us will make us stagnant and vulnerable."

Stagnant and vulnerable? "I still don't know what you mean."

"Have you heard that humans weren't created by anyone?"

"I heard that many humans think their ancestors were created by someone, but they can't agree who did it, and many scientists think none of the hypothesized creators of humanity ever existed and humanity arose through a natural process. What would that have to do with Jakob making us stagnant and vulnerable?"

He took a very deep breath before explaining. "While I was training for this job, I decided to look up several human books on biology. Many of them referred to a process called evolution, whereby species adapt to their environments, generation by generation. When they reproduce, mutations are common. Some mutations grant advantages over others of the same species and enable the carrier to reproduce more and spread the gene throughout the population. For this reason, I started the policy of leaving harmless mutations in our cloning process alone.

Previously, any mutation was corrected. However many species, such as humans, do not generally reproduce by cloning. They reproduce sexually, blending half their genes at random with those of another individual. This introduces an additional form of variation into the population and adds another form of competition as individuals compete to mate with individuals of the opposite gender." He drew in another deep breath before continuing. "Humans still prefer to reproduce sexually. Therefore, they have the potential to evolve much more quickly than we do and gain an advantage over us."

I thought that I could almost understand now. "You think that Jakob was wrong to hide the results of my findings."

He nodded.

"But what about the reasons he gave for doing that? Keeping the Protectors' Clans in line and preventing overpopulation?"

Maximus uttered a sound half like a snort and half like a laugh. "After he told me about that, I looked up the actual human population growth rates. It appears that just a few generations after the mortality rate of a human population drops, enabling rapid growth, the birth rate tapers off. It's like they make lots of babies when they think many of them won't survive to adulthood, but after things change so that all their young can expect to grow up, they voluntarily sterilize themselves, temporarily or permanently, to limit the number of children they have to raise." He let that sink in before addressing my former point. "As for 'keeping the Clans in line', can you honestly say they are under control after what just happened to your friends?"

I thought about it. "No, they're not." At that point, I

decided that I could trust Maximus Griggs with the secret I so badly needed to keep from Jakob Griggs and the entire Marquez Clan. "Almost a week before I started working for the Society for the Preservation of Parahuman Species, I was attacked by a bounty hunter. Marquez drones stopped him, but afterwards, a commander, Derrick Marquez, spoke to me. He told me that my group would now be paying three times the rate we were already paying and that if I refused or attempted to get insurance with another Clan, he would release videos portraying us performing certain acts that might impair our ability to earn a living." I was not yet inclined to elaborate on me and Aniya's activities to this person. "I agreed, and shortly after, I took a job with the SPPS because I'd heard they could convince the Clans to lower my rates and I could even make some extra cash to help out my friends. However, the night before the incident, they told me that ever since I joined the SPPS, their already exorbitant rates had been increasing by leaps and bounds. Even with me contributing my income, it was reaching levels that they couldn't afford. So they decided to have a chat with Derrick Marquez about their rates and, if necessary, persuade him violently." I ducked my head between my legs and covered my face so that Maximus wouldn't see my expression of grief. "Then the negotiations apparently went wrong, and either Denal snapped and killed Aniya and Cole, or Marquez didn't like their terms and killed Aniya and Cole for it. I want to believe that my only surviving friend isn't an insane murderer, but I'm so inclined to doubt everything that I wouldn't be too surprised if he was."

I looked up long enough to see Max's jaw hanging wide open in shock. "By the makers," he said, "I didn't realize it ran that deep." He straightened up and asked me another question that would shake me like nothing in my short life had before: "Was the rate hike after you started working here, or after you found a mutation that would enable us to breed?"

I tensed up. "Cole actually said that the big increase was a few days before, and it was less than a week after I discovered the MOR10X-6 promoter inhibition."

It was then that he dropped the bombshell that would shape the remainder of my years to come. "I think my father ordered your friends killed."

I collapsed, falling backwards and hitting my head on the rocky ground I had been sitting on. This was too much. I was shocked back to reality by Maximus pinching my toes between his claws. "What makes you say that?!" I demanded.

"Well," he began, stroking his chin in thought, "a few hours after your meeting with him my progenitor invited Jerome Marquez and all eight of his clones to dinner with him." Good to know he didn't put all that food to waste, then. "And I suspect that when you asked the Marquez officers about what had happened, the only reason you weren't taken in for questioning was that you worked for the SPPS."

I thought of how that tiger had grabbed me and demanded I tell him where Denal had scurried off to, and how he let me go after Derrick had told him that I was "with Griggs." I sat up and said, "Yes, that's accurate."

The savannah cat grabbed my hand and pulled me the rest of the way forward. "I think he was trying to demonstrate how powerful he was. Even if you didn't catch on that he was responsible for the extreme actions of the Marquez, you would realize that he had some measure of control over the Protectors' Guilds when you were exempt from questioning during a murder investigation involving your closest companions."

I considered his words carefully. Yes, it did seem odd that a few words were able to dissuade such an aggressive enforcer from strangling me. But I hadn't even considered the possibility that Jakob Griggs had orchestrated the murders and framing for murders of my friends. I could believe that he had convinced the Marquez's to raise my friends' premiums in order to give himself more leverage over me and convince me to keep the mutation a secret, but killing them seemed a bit much. And I told Maximus such.

"Maybe he didn't mean to kill them," the clone told me, "but that would still make him responsible in part for your friends' deaths. There has to be justice for what he did."

Justice? "How would you bring about this justice?"

At this, he grinned. The same toothy grin that had so intimidated me when sported by his father. "We strip him of his power and help parahumanity evolve, that's how." I looked at him incredulously, still unable to figure out what he was talking about. Then he added, "I kept a backup of the genetic data you showed me. We can make it open-source."

I finally got it. "And then every biochemist in the solar system will be able to grant parahumans the ability to make babies, and he'll have no influence over the cloneclans." And then I recalled what else he had said about his influence. "But then the Clans will be unrestrained. What will keep them from abusing the people like Marquez did to us before I even joined this whole mess with the SPPS?"

Maximus looked like he hadn't a clue; apparently he hadn't thought that far ahead. "Well, I'm sure there are better systems of governance than the feudalism we've apparently developed into. Maybe I could read some human works on government, and if the Guilds are cruel to enough people we can convince them to start a revolution to put in place something better."

"I don't recommend corporatocracy," I added with a bit of snark. I'd left Ceres for a reason, damn it.

"Look, I'll leave it up to you whether to release it." He pushed the rock covering our containment suits aside and retrieved them. As he handed me my suit, he said, "I'd suggest you take the rest of the work week off. You're no good to us if you're still grieving over your friends. You'll be paid as if you were still here at work."

I started to throw on the suit (no point to walking all the way to the lockers naked) when a data card fell out. I picked it up. There was no label, but I could guess what was stored on it.

The chip was indeed what I had suspected: all the information on MOR10X-6 I had found, the sequence, the phenotype, the mutation that disabled it, everything. I spent the next day researching what it would cost to produce a mutagen that would induce the mutation. It was only a few qcoins, and a CRISPR enzyme to remove the gene entirely didn't cost much more. I found several different biotechnology blogs and open-source libraries where I could upload the data and distribute it to anyone who cared enough to read it.

I thought about how the Belt would handle this information. The cloneclans and wealthy oligarchs who had families already would benefit the most, as they had more copies of their genes to spread already. But now that I thought about it, if we still could reproduce only by cloning, such people would be the entirety of parahumanity in about a century. If I sent out the formula, their genelines would be a minority of the total population. And no doubt the powerful could lose power when they had millions of potential competitors.

And I thought of my friends, dead or on the run, thanks to one man who would lose everything with just a few taps of a button.

One by one, I sent my findings to a dozen different sites. Tab by tab, key by key, I signed the death warrant for a civilization and hopefully the birth certificate of a new species.

Chapter 12

The effects of the upload were drastic. Within days, the blogosphere was erupting with opinions on the revelation. Most believed that it was fake. I couldn't really blame them, as it was a rather immense change and posted by someone virtually unknown. The fact that my only notable claim to fame was arriving on Vesta with a price on my head and being the only member of my group who wasn't currently dead or on the run from the Protectors' Guilds wouldn't help me much, I decided, so I uploaded the data under a pseudonym. The following comes from one of the more notable forum threads on the subject, where I wrote under another pseudonym, "GoldFoxie":

Genotypist: This has to be fake, you'd think that if it were this easy the asteroids would be crawling with mutant cubs by now.

BioStick: Not to mention that we're all blends of DNA from multiple species. It would have to be almost impossible for us to breed.

GoldFoxie: @Genotypist: Not if the information was locked up by the corps. I work at the SPPS and you'd be surprised how often we run into "clearance required" when running sequences through the old corporate databanks. @BioStick: You do know that anthropomorphic parahumans are over 99% human while uplifted parahumans have nearly all of their genes from a single species, right?

RedBull: @GoldFoxie: If you're so sure that the mutagen works, why don't you take it yourself and get pregnant or get someone else pregnant?

GoldFoxie: @RedBull: Once I get some testes or ovaries, I will. Why don't you try it out?

Private message from admin@GeneHack.net: GoldFoxie, we have traced your ISP and determined it to be the same one that the data on the fertility restoration originated from. Under board rules, you are required to write about your findings under the same tag that you posted them under. This rule helps to ensure our rule of transparency. While we do not object to the use of pseudonyms to publish data, we encourage researchers to take responsibility for their works instead of hiding behind other names to influence public reactions to their achievements.

Seriously? They didn't mind false names so long as you used the same fake name everywhere? How hypocritical was that? I did not dare post on that forum again, but I returned a few hours later to see what had sprung up. Sure enough, the worst:

admin@GeneHack.net: ISP trace has identified user GoldFoxie as user DarwinRevolution, author of the fertility genehack project.

Genotypist: That figures.

RedBull: Of course zie was trying to further their practical joke. And what other reason would a neuter have for publishing a means to reproduce by sex?

HoundOfGod: @RedBull: Isn't it obvious? What other genderless foxes are there that work for the SPPS and are named after a "precious" metal who have appeared in the news recently? I'll give you a hint. (He linked to video about my friends' deaths.) *Clearly zie has a grudge against the Cloneclans and wants to break their exclusive access to genetic perpetuation, even if zie can't benefit from the treatment personally. Me and my partner are having the CRISPR protein synthesized as I type this. If it works I will chronicle the progress.*

I dropped the tablet in shock. This HoundOfGod character, whoever they were, had just exposed me. What gave them the right to do that?

But on the other hand, (1) it lent me a bit of credibility, (2) they were trying out the more hazardous version of the treatment, and (3) clearly they did not like the Cloneclans. Perhaps they could be an ally in the coming revolution that Maximus was talking about. I would have to ask Max about them the next time I saw him.

The following Monday, I came back to work. Cautious that someone might recognize me from the Internet, I took the less traveled paths to the building and wore a concealing trench coat with a hologram that replaced my face with that of a red fox. As I was preparing to don my containment suit, a familiar-looking savannah cat wearing a black robe followed into the decontamination chamber.

"Oh, Maximus, I was just looking for-" I cut myself off as I realized that it was not Maximus Griggs but rather his progenitor, with a rather displeased look on his face. "Jakob, sorry; I was expecting your son."

"Was he the one who put you up to this?!" He demanded, angrily. "Did he tell you to release the information about that gene so he could wrest control from me?!"

"No," I said somewhat untruthfully, "it was my decision after two of my friends were murdered by one of the Protectors you claimed you kept in line."

"What exactly are you implying, Argentum?"

"I'm saying that if some Marquez killed my friends

over high coverage rates, that tells me that either you lack the control over the Clans that you claim to have," I sucked in a breath and fiddled with some of my vest buttons as I spoke to him "or you ordered their deaths yourself."

He looked slightly surprised at my statement, but not overly so. "What makes you say that?"

I straightened up and started to circle slowly around to the exit while keeping my distance from him, trying my best to keep any trace of fear from my voice and actions but failing to prevent an edge of anger from creeping in. "You told me that you were preventing the Clans from acting like feudal nobles!"

"I did," he admitted. "But I can't be held responsible for every little thing they do. I may have told Marquez to increase your friends' rates a little, but I did not expect them to get violent. It's not my fault if he had to defend himself."

"He had cyanide darts," I replied. "He could have used less-than-lethal paralytics, but he shot them with enough poison to kill a baseline elephant." Then I thought of something else he was undeniably responsible for. "And your clones enabled the Guild leaders to make their own allies and cement their positions in place. You and your progenitor are the whole reason why the Protectors' Guilds are known as Houses and Clans in pop culture."

"I wouldn't give the original Griggs too much credit. The discounts for the Guild leaders were my idea. He wanted to charge everyone the same price and even offer financing for lower-income parahumans. He thought my idea would reduce the genetic diversity of the asteroid to levels that were somehow dangerous. That was why he had to go."

I stared at him in horror. "You killed your own father?!"

"It's not like I shot or stabbed him. A few loose bolts in his personal shuttle, a few holes in his spacesuit, some loose wires in his radio… All I needed to do was make a fatal accident a little more possible, and he was as good as dead."

He turned as if he had suddenly realized something. "And now that you know that, you should probably die as well." He began to draw something from under his robe.

"And if the one who brought down your monopoly dies suddenly, what do you think the blogs will say?" I asked. He stopped and stared at me as I continued. "As it is, most people seem to think that the mutation is a joke. Of course that will change once the first few babies are born, but I suspect that my death would convince some of the skeptics that there truly is something to my research."

"Fine." He released the handle of whatever weapon he had and instead pulled out a mini-tablet. As he scrolled down the menu, he said, "Your employment with the Society for the Preservation of Parahuman Species is now terminated. If you are seen within 100 meters of this building again, our in-house security will shoot to kill." He showed me the screen that now listed my employment status as "terminated". "Now get out."

I picked up my trenchcoat and threw it back on. As I left, I looked at one of the buttons on my vest, in particular the blinking light on the back side.

To: HoundOfGod
From: GoldFoxie
Subject: You should find this interesting

This is Argentum, you know, the one you more or less exposed yesterday? You didn't have any right to do that. I was fired and almost killed by Jakob Griggs. I realize that eventually the secret would have come out, but I would have preferred at least a week to make a run for it before my life was truly in danger.

That said, I see the value of having someone such as yourself on my side, especially as you are testing out my project yourself. I wish the best of luck to you and your partner.

Attached is a video I recorded earlier today. I hope that you will feature it on your blog tonight.

Chapter 13

The next day, the planetoid erupted into chaos. There were riots in the streets. Protesters gathered outside the SPPS and the Protectors' offices. I stayed in my apartment, having no desire to go out on the streets Odds were that someone would recognize me and either hang me (as difficult as that would be in this gravity) or fawn over me. Neither option was particularly appealing.

It was while I sat there, watching the chaos I had wrought, that I was caught off guard.

One minute, I was lying back watching the riots and attempting to hide under the covers while keeping my eyes just barely uncovered; the next, a team of assassins in camo-suits were materializing in my bedroom. As the mixed-species team surrounded me and attempted to grab me, I drew my gun, which I had hidden under a pillow after Jakob threatened me, and squeezed off three shots as I attempted to dive for the window. The first shot hit one of the assassins-what looked like a bear or a large cat, I couldn't really tell-in the chest, but the other two went wide as the explosions issuing from the barrel threw me against the wall. I was momentarily stunned by the impact, giving one of the thugs enough time to shove a drug spray into my mouth.

I felt a faint sting for a moment as the nanoparticles burrowed into the roof of my muzzle, then numbness began to spread across my face. I made a brief attempt to make a subvocal call, but I couldn't feel my jaw anymore. Then my vision blurred. I felt myself slipping away. Before succumbing to unconsciousness, I saw the hit team open a bag made of active camo material and one of the massive parahumans dragging me towards it.

After what felt like just moments, I came to in the bag. It was dark and rough with power cords lining the interior and digging into my sides. I started to struggle, attempting to wiggle my way out of the narrow hole, when I was unceremoniously dumped out onto a metal bed. Two guards held my arms and legs down while a feline of some sort dressed in surgical scrubs poked me in the throat with a pair of sharp needles. I felt my body course with an electrical shock and heard a snap and pop of frying circuitry. Willing myself to breathe again once my limbs stopped twitching, I demanded, still somewhat numbly, "Whaaa?"

"My more obedient son here just disabled your subvocal implant," I heard a rather unpleasantly familiar voice state. "Octavius was more inclined toward the medical practices, though he had some trouble passing the surgeon's guild entry exam–something about his ethics."

The doctor next to me, whose serval spots I could now discern underneath his mask, snorted as if his progenitor had said something funny. "Yeah, he had a little chat with the entry board. Now I help him out whenever he needs some chop-shop work done."

And Maximus came from this gene pool? I was starting

to wonder if someone had spiked his biofab tank with something. "What do you want now?"

Jakob's face suddenly popped into my field of vision. "I thought about what you said," he told me. "You said that if you died after revealing the big secret, it would lend credibility to the idea that your treatment worked. And then you put a video of me threatening you online. Now I'm thinking that I need to limit the damage you can do by making you disappear entirely."

The thugs picked me up and carried me over to a large metallic cylinder with a hatch on the side. "This," Jakob continued, "is a canister for the mass driver that was built here on Vesta during the last few years of the corporate era. It was never used, but it would have shot steel cans full of ore back to Earth for processing."

The two goons dropped me into the cylinder and started to shut the lid. I attempted to scramble out before it was closed, but all that accomplished was a heavy steel door slamming on my right hand. I let out a yelp in pain, and they opened it just enough for me to pull my hand back in. I couldn't see the damage but I could feel blood oozing out, and I was pretty sure some bones were broken.

I could faintly hear Jakob Grigg's voice through the cylinder wall. "Now, I don't want Earth thinking we're attacking them, so I placed explosive bolts along the seams that will tear the cylinder apart an hour or two out. But you'll keep going along your pre-programmed trajectory until you reach Earth. I'm pretty sure you'll be long dead by the time you are cremated in Earth's atmosphere."

I seethed with rage at Jakob's speech. "Seems a bit over-complicated Griggs. Planning a new career as a spy movie villain?"

"No, I just want you to suffer for almost ruining me like this," he replied punctually.

Then I felt the cylinder moving as it was conveyed into the loading chamber of the giant railgun that the corporations had intended to use for sending the Belt's wealth back home. I crouched down in what I hoped was the rear of the cylinder and waited for it to fire. There was no bang, no explosion like my gun emitted, just a sudden acceleration that pushed me back into the wall. It felt like it liquefied my organs. I realized seconds later that that wasn't quite the case. I was still alive, for one thing.

I floated, weightless now that the acceleration was over, in the cylinder. I couldn't see a thing, but I felt my way forward, pushing myself off the back wall gently. When I came to the opposite side, I stopped myself with my hand, forgetting that I'd crushed it minutes earlier. Pain shot up my arm, and I suspect that a few of the fast-forming scabs that my augmented platelets had formed (bleeding is a tad more serious in microgravity or a sealed spacesuit than it is on Earth, you know) broke open. I cradled my arm as I drifted slowly back. I guess air resistance slowed me down to a near standstill, because I found myself floating in empty space. I still couldn't see anything, but I could breathe still, so I guessed I was somewhere in the middle of the giant can, and it still hadn't exploded.

I took a moment to think about my situation. I had been naked when they captured me, so I had none of my usual wearable electronics to signal for help. I tried to use my subvocal comm and got a nasty shock for my efforts; apparently Jakob was telling the truth about having fried my implant.

So I was drifting somewhere in the middle of space, on

a ballistic path to Earth, in a can with no life support that was going to explode in a few minutes, with no way to call for help. I'm pretty sure I broke down sobbing at some point. I don't know how long it took–there were no clocks, and when your life is in danger, time has a habit of passing extremely slowly–but it felt like I was crying for hours.

Eventually I got a hold of myself and started contemplating my situation. There had been no question that I was going to die someday, I had just hoped that my death would be a lot later than now. I could survive maybe an hour after the pod broke apart, conscious for most of that time, and this cylinder had maybe a couple hours' worth of oxygen in it. Too bad it was set to blow in one more hour.

What would happen next, I wondered? Burning up in the atmosphere of a planet I had never known but had given rise to my ancestors, I supposed. But I wouldn't be able to witness my meteoric cremation–my brain would have shut down. What would dying be like? I had never subscribed to any religious beliefs, but I knew that some humans thought that at death, their consciousness separated from their body somehow and moved to another universe of some kind, where they gained a new body and were either rewarded or punished for eternity according to how they had lived their previous life. Others believed that your consciousness was transferred to a new-born organism at death, so you had a new chance to achieve some form of enlightenment, whatever that meant. And of course, many others believed that there was nothing after death; your brain simply shut down for good, and that was that.

I was starting to think that death would be like simply

falling into a deep dreamless sleep from which you would never wake...

Then the can burst open. There were blinding flashes of light above and below me that blew away the ends of the cylinder, followed by streaks of flame running down the walls. The body of the cylinder flew away in four separate directions. I looked ahead of me; the view was nothing but stars, burning away in the endless night. If I craned my neck a little, I could see the sun—a big, blinding ball of yellow light. I chose to look at the stars again, just hanging there.

I recalled that most elements heavier than helium were formed when stars exploded in supernovae. I was pretty sure that most of my body was composed of heavier elements, which must have meant that countless stars had to die for me to ever come into being. I thought of what would happen to the atoms that made up every molecule of my being. No doubt most of the organic compounds that composed the vast majority of my body would be burned off into water and carbon dioxide, which might be absorbed by some plant, which would be eaten by a cow or something that would be cut up into steaks for some human or maybe a rich parahuman. I would be part of another thinking being, but my memories, my personality, what made me distinct from everyone else, would be gone.

I was so wrapped up in my morbid thoughts that I almost didn't notice the harpoon streaking past me, a glint of light that shot out to my left, then retracted. I was still trying to think of what it had been when the second harpoon struck me in the small of my back. There was a stabbing pain, and suddenly a large spear point jutted out of my stomach, or rather through my liver on the opposite side. Prongs extended from the sides of the point, and it pulled me back towards the source of the intruding weapon. What was going on now? Had Jakob Griggs changed his mind and decided that death by massive organ damage was worse than a slow death from anoxia?

I was still wondering as the airlock doors closed in front of me. Then a suited parahuman glided up to me and detached the head of the harpoon from the cable, pulling it the rest of the way through me. Looking at the gaping hole in my belly, they pulled another of those familiar spray bottles out and gave me a squirt in the mouth. This time I happily accepted the sweet embrace of unconsciousness.

When I came to, I was tied down on a zero-g bed with a series of tubes sticking out of me. One notable tube was covering the giant hole in my gut. Above me hung an octopoid assembly of shining plastic arms. I could have sworn it was an autodoctor, but those were ludicrously expensive; only big-time executives on Earth could afford them, or maybe Griggs could.

Hence my surprise when instead of a sadistic savannah cat a bleary-eyed red panda rushed up to my side.

"Denal?!" I shouted in his face. Well, it didn't sound like shouting to me, but I reviewed the video later. He started rapidly moving his mouth like he was talking but no words were coming out. "Speak up! I can't hear a word you're saying!"

He looked shocked at my statement. Then he seemed to remember something, drew out a pair of augmented reality glasses, and held them out to me. I reached out with my left hand (my right appeared to be encased in some sort of device) and put them on. Denal made the mouth movements again and text appeared in my field of view. "Okay, can you hear–I mean see–my words now?"

"I can read the text on these glasses! What is going on?!"

His mouth made some more movements, followed by more text on the lenses. "Your eardrums suffered damage from the sudden exposure to vacuum. You're lucky the gengineers strengthened our lungs, or you wouldn't even be able to speak."

"Where am I?" It didn't make much sense for Jakob to hire Denal to keep me alive after nearly killing me. Was he a prisoner too?

"Don't you recognize your own ship, Argentum?" More text, but Denal's mouth wasn't moving. He turned towards the door and I followed his gaze to see another one of the parahumans I least expected to see: it was Olga Wolf, the vigilante who had saved our lives on our first day in Vesta, or maybe one of her sisters. "Of course," she said, "I made some modifications after my house bought it from the Marquez Clan. Though I suppose, since you and panda boy here are technically part owners, we shouldn't have been able to buy it at all. Probably why we got it so cheap."

"What do you want?!" I demanded. If she was working for Jakob she was certainly going to a lot of trouble just to punish me.

She cringed a little at my words. "Stop shouting. I know you're deaf but that doesn't mean we can't hear you perfectly fine." Shouting? "Anyway, didn't you ever wonder just who HoundOfGod was?"

"You?" I asked incredulously, trying to sound a bit softer this time. "The rebellious clone of one of the major Clans is the net activist who believed me immediately?"

Then I thought of something. "Wait, if you're HoundOfGod, then that means you've tried out the treatment. Does it work?"

She smiled a bit at my inquiry. "The autodoc suggests that it'll be a month before my first oogenesis cycle and Denal's spermatogenesis are complete. I guess we'll know then."

I blinked a couple times in shock. "Wait, you and Denal?!" Figures that lech would be one of the first parahumans to father a child.

Denal's fur stood up in embarrassment. "It's sort of a long story." He said.

I gestured with the machine covering my right wrist to the hose leading into my guts. "I've got nowhere to go for… how long will I be hooked up to these things, anyway?" I addressed the question to Olga. It was her equipment, after all.

"The bioprinter will take about a week to complete your new liver, gallbladder, pancreas, and lengths of large and small intestine." She looked sorry about the massive damage her harpoon had to inflict in order to save my life. "Your cochleal implants and prosthetic hand should be ready in a couple more hours, though."

Prosthetic? I looked back down at the thing where my right hand should have been, and it occurred to me that I couldn't feel that hand at all. The damage must have been more severe than I had noticed. I tried to head off any thoughts about the loss of my hand by changing the subject. "So, how did you two end up together?"

"Well," Denal said before Olga could say anything more, "after I was framed for two counts of murder, I ran as fast as I could for Wolf territory. A few minutes later, I was caught by two of their drones and a ridiculously muscular coyote enforcer. They took me back to their base, and one of her sisters told me that they were considering extraditing me to either Marquez or Ceres. Thinking fast, I gave her the camera hidden in my button and told them to review the evidence."

Olga gave a sound that could have been a loud scoff; the Augmented Reality glasses couldn't make it out. "Please," she said sarcastically (the AR glasses highlighted the tone). "He babbled incomprehensibly for five minutes, insisting he was innocent until we pulled him into a holding cell. We discovered the camera while picking over his stuff for anything valuable." She snickered a little before continuing. "I managed to convince my mother that we could tick Marquez off royally if we kept him here."

"Right." Denal interjected. "Anyway, after I proved my innocence with the Wolfs, they put me to work maintaining their fleet of vehicles. The next day, Olga showed me the video she had made with my material and asked me if I was interested in helping her 'tear down this rotted foundation of a civilization', or something like that."

"So that's all?" I asked Olga. "You're just doing this"– referring to the whole trying to-get-him-to-knock-her-up thing–"to express your views on Vestan politics?"

"Well, he is pretty good in bed," the she-wolf admitted. Denal grinned. "But yes, the clone-entrenched administrators of justice with no accountability need to be brought down. Including my mother and sisters, I'm afraid."

I realized I had one more question to ask of them before I could go back to sleep and recover. "How did you find me anyways?"

"I have a backdoor into the Marquez network. I've been using it to keep tabs on you since Denal went into hiding. We noticed when the cameras and IR sensors went dark along a certain path leading from your apartment to the mass driver loading bay." Olga parted the fur at the base of her neck to show me a capped brain-computer interface port–very difficult to learn how to use, but immensely useful for complex computer work. "Mom shouldn't have prepared me to do all the electronics stuff in the racketeering business."

Chapter 14

I spent most of the week it took to print out my new vital organs trying to learn how to use my new hand. I assure you it is not like the movies. By the end of that week, I was able to open and close it, but more complex gestures were still nearly impossible to perform. My nerves and brain simply couldn't rewire themselves any faster. The autodoc stapled the severed ends of the nerves in my wrist to the control circuits of the new hand, but it was still vastly different from my organic hand, and there was nothing they could do. Once the last chunk of liver was in place, surgical micro-bots stitched everything together at the cellular level, leaving nothing but a tender bald spot on my abdomen. It hurt to stand up but Denal and Olga decided it was time for me to appear before the public regardless.

While I had been getting pieced back together, Jakob Griggs' memetic engineers had been hard at work spreading the idea that my treatment was a fake. Like he had said, they were capitalizing on the fact that I had disappeared without a trace to discredit the research I had presented. It was known that a few dozen people had synthesized and used the treatment after HoundOfGod's endorsement, but since it took a month for the effects to become apparent, many of them now doubted that it had done anything but make them feel ill for a few days. There was a slim chance that eventually some of them would become pregnant by sheer accident and the treatment would catch on, but for now, it looked like the very concept of parahuman fertility would be relegated to the waste basket of pseudo-science. There needed to be drastic action, now.

So the very day my surgeries were completed, Olga set up her recording gear in my infirmary to stream a very special installment of her blog. It would be streamed live that evening as they were recording, with questions from viewers that I would be able to answer. As the appointed time drew near, I sat up on the bed, still wearing my patient's gown. They thought that emphasizing the abuse I had taken might stir sympathy.

As the seconds on the clock ticked down, Olga went through the last couple steps to start the stream. She'd start with her usual black screen accompanied by voiceover and subtitles explaining the video to come and then switch over to me. I would tell her viewers everything. "We are starting in three, two..." Olga's announced, then she switched on a distortion unit that would make her sound like the net revolutionary's distinctive gravelly tones.

"This is HoundOfGod. It has been over a week since our last broadcast and no doubt some of you are wondering why I haven't been covering the recent disturbances surrounding the revelation that parahuman sterility is easily fixed. You may have concluded that the complete disappearance of Argentum, known by the net aliases DarwinRevolution and GoldFoxie, the author of the paper detailing the gene the corporations used to prevent us from reproducing, had something to do with it. Or you may have concluded that when I failed to make a baby with my partner, I hid myself away in shame like many of others who tried the treatment did. To those who believe the latter, I recommend reading some basic information on how meiosis works and waiting a month like we're doing. The former is closer to the truth. You see, Argentum did not completely disappear."

A map of the Marquez cavern's sensors appeared in the field of view. A clearly defined path was utterly devoid of sensor sweep symbols. "For about twenty minutes on the day of the riots, a set of Marquez sensors went dark. As you can see, the specific sensors were too convenient to be coincidental, as one end of the path they form is at Argentum's apartment complex."

The image changed to an interior view of my apartment, the sheets disheveled and the appliances thrown around and broken. There were even a few splatters of blood. "Zir apartment was later reported by the landlord to be in a state of disarray. He found blood staining the floor and a 3D printed M1911 semiautomatic pistol, similar to the one Argentum was known to carry."

A picture of me at the time of the bounty hunter incident appeared alongside the apartment, with a circle and arrow around my holster. The apartment view zoomed in on the same gun lying on the floor. "There were also two bullets of the caliber used in the firearm embedded in one of the walls of the apartment, as well as three spent casings on the floor near the gun. This suggests that Argentum had been attacked and managed to pull off three shots before zie was captured, one of which hit one of the aggressors. The other end of the path was just as interesting, it turned out."

The still images changed views to a gaping metal hole in the side of the planetoid, going down into darkness. "The mass driver, a never-used project of the old corporations that would have saved them billions on shipping back to Earth. I drew the obvious conclusion and took a ship out along the trajectory the driver would have fired upon. What I found was no less than miraculous."

The view now changed to a still picture of open space, which zoomed in on a tiny spot until the screen was filled with my furry black and white ass. "The broken and bleeding body of our great unsung hero, Argentum. Imagine my shock to find zir all the way out there without so much as a spacesuit."

The view then changed to me being pulled into the cargo bay with the help of a suited Olga, conveniently cut off above the harpoon in my gut. "Imagine my relief to see that zie had held onto life for that long."

Now it showed me unconscious, lying on the medical bed with a gas mask over my face and the autodoc reaching into the assorted holes in me. "Regardless, zie was in critical condition and required extensive surgery and organ replacement before zie could return to Vesta. But now zie is ready to make zir first public appearance. I am transferring the feed now to zir hospital bed on board my ship so zie can tell zir story and later answer your questions."

The video changed to me, and I straightened up suddenly, which shot a surge of pain up my torso, causing me to reflexively clutch at my side with my right hand. Unfortunately, as that hand was now a barely functional prosthesis, that only made it worse. Self-conscious that I was being watched by possibly hundreds of parahumans, I slowly moved my hand back down onto the bed.

"All right," I began. "For those of you who didn't obsessively look me up and go over every little detail of my life, I'll give you the basics." I retold the whole story, how we had fled Ceres, how we found difficulty paying the Marquez Guild's rates and I sought employment with the SPPS. How I'd discovered the mutation and how Jakob Griggs had convinced me to keep it secret. And then my friends had been killed or framed for murder.

As I began to wrap up my tale I turned back to pry open my new hand and held it up to the camera. "As for this, well, when I returned to work Jakob threatened to kill me, but I convinced him that killing me would help validate my claim that parahuman infertility was easy to fix. Then I suppose I did the stupid thing and uploaded the video of him threatening me. That got him angry enough to try to make me 'disappear' in the most painful possible way."

I shook my wrist waving my fake hand around. "My right hand was crushed in the process of cramming me into a giant railgun cylinder." I leaned forward and pointed a mechanical finger down my ear. "Both eardrums burst when the cylinder exploded in open space causing rapid decompression." I swept my gown to the side showing off the bald spot where the bulk of the organ transplants had taken place. "Liver, pancreas, gallbladder, and five centimeters of intestine; wrecked when HoundOfGod, a.k.a. Olga Wolf, the rebellious clone princess-"

"Now wait a second!" Olga cut in, not even bothering with the distortion this time.

"You expose me, I expose you. It's only fair," I told her, motioning to the right of the camera where she sat. "Now, as I was saying, my internal organs were destroyed when Olga was forced to reel me in with a harpoon through the gut. Now, I want to make it clear that I do not blame her; the ship didn't have any other methods of grabbing a small, fast-moving object such as myself. But still I was resigned to a slow death from anoxia followed by an impromptu cremation in Earth's atmosphere when I felt a massive stabbing–no–impaling pain."

I moved my gown back into place and lay back on the bed. "So that's my story. Any questions?"

Within seconds of the comment box going active, the feed was loaded with questions, as well as the usual troll comments that inevitably appear on any online discussion. I ignored the ones that didn't actually ask a question. Unfortunately, the first real question that I could answer happened to be "Why are you so obsessed with sex, you neuter?"

"Obsessed with sex?" I replied incredulously. "Well, I can't say that I'm obsessed with sex. But I do believe that it will become necessary for us to survive as a species. Not only does reproduction by cloning give tyrants like Jakob a focal point to seize, but it reduces the ability of our kind to evolve."

I prepared for another long lecture, recalling what Maximus had told me. I explained the basics of sexual reproduction in relation to evolution. "In addition, cloning is expensive and therefore limited to a narrow percentage of the population. This means that within a few generations, the parahuman population would be limited to a few dozen genotypes rather than the hundreds of thousands we have now. Jakob Griggs actually told me that he took measures to make sure that only the extremely wealthy could continue their genelines."

As I glanced over the rest of the comments, one stuck out in particular. "Speaking of sex, why don't you share some of your nocturnal activities with that wolf-possum 'friend' of yours?"

I read that over and over again in disbelief. Who would know about that? I glanced at Denal, who was fussing over a computer readout. He shook his head and showed me the circuitry diagram displayed on his tablet. Then I remembered someone else who knew.

"Nocturnal activities? Wait a minute. Is that you, Derrick Marquez?!" I yelled at the camera, my voice full of fury. "Why don't you share your own nocturnal activities with Aniya, like pumping her full of cellular poison and dumping her limp carcass into the back of your van?!"

Immediately, the other commenters turned on the "guest " who had brought up my and Aniya's proclivities–things like "Wait, she was zir lover?" and, "You killed zir girlfriend, no wonder zie hates the Guild feudal system so much", and "Run an ISP trace on that bastard so we can beat him up!" The one I was positive was Derrick by now tried to deflect the net rage by going into detail on the things he was accusing me of, but that mostly served to attract more sympathy, especially once the video he had threatened to post was linked to and people saw me retreat into Aniya's pouch out of fright. Apparently, it gave many of them the impression that Aniya and I were a loving couple rather than just a pair of perverts.

Then, amongst the flame war, there appeared one question that I found myself having difficulty answering. "If you are neuter, than how can you benefit from reversing sterility? You have no reproductive organs to repair."

"Well, I might be able to find a way to print and graft fully functional reproductive organs to myself someday," was my immediate answer. "Failing that, I might make one last clone who has been modified to have a sex."

"You should clone Aniya," stated another comment. I refused to even acknowledge that comment, but it got me thinking.

Clone Aniya. I thought to myself. *I do have samples of her DNA, but what would I do with a clone of her? Raise her as my daughter and slip into her pouch every other night? That sounds a bit creepy, don't you think?*

There were many more questions, but I don't believe there was anywhere near that much drama at any other point during the rest of the video, and I didn't care to remember any of it.

Chapter 15

Derrick Marquez was jumped by a smart mob as he attempted to leave the apartment he had been using to access the network. He tried to slip past in a camosuit, but the mob was too large and he brushed against too many people. Before they swarmed him and tore the suit off, he managed to shoot a few mob members, fortunately with normal paralytics, but they did find several darts loaded with cyanide and nastier toxins such as sarin, which, rather than simply disabling them like the tetrodotoxin favored by Olga, destroyed nerve endings and condemned parahumans to a slow, lingering death from asphyxiation like the one I had faced in the vacuum of space, or at best a life of drastically limited mobility.

Regardless, many considered the mere possession of such toxins ample justification for the rather creative hanging they gave him, dropping him off the roof of a ceiling-scraper with some weights tied to his ankles and a rope just two meters short of the building's height tied around his neck. It would have been considered overkill anywhere with even one percent of Earth's gravity. Derrick's death was but one of many suffered by the Protectors' Guilds all over Vesta. Unfortunately, the Guilds responded in kind, enforcers brutally bashing in the skulls of protestors and filling them with neurotoxins, sometimes of the fatal variety.

Amidst all this chaos, Jakob Griggs had withdrawn the SPPS into their headquarters and fortified it with armed guards and auto-turrets. After the first few rioters were gunned down, they generally left the place alone, the king in his castle under siege.

Meanwhile, we ourselves hunkered down at the spaceport. Olga had apparently been planning to hide us in Wolf territory, but now that her Clan knew that she was the notorious blogger HoundOfGod, they had made it quite clear that she was no longer welcome at home. Guess I'd screwed up a bit there. Olga had modified the ship to include a pair of retractable mini-turrets flanking the primary airlock to either side. They fended off the first attempt at invasion by a Marquez SWAT team quite adequately.

The turrets did not need to face a second invasion, though. Shortly after that first attempt, a group of supporters began to gather around the entrance to our ship, most of them heavily armed with a wide variety of different weapons, everything from improvised clubs made from pipes to automatic Gauss rifles. With the abundance of hardware and people between us and the Guilds, we decided it was necessary to disable the auto-fire on our turrets. We kept the manual override in easy reach, but now we could get someone to remove the bodies from the first assault.

There were two more attempts by what appeared to be mostly Marquez troops to gain entrance to our sanctum, but the improvised militia before us drove them back both times. I'm sorry to say that there were losses incurred on our side, among them a ferret who caught a stray bullet in the neck and a bull who took a cosh straight through his lower jaw and into his brainpan. Still, this seemed to bolster their resolve. More and more flocked to our side, setting up fortifications and portable shelters in the cave that served as the main reception area of the port. It was starting to resemble a military encampment as the population of the spaceport reached the hundreds.

Every so often, I left the safety of the ship to walk among the followers I had never intended to gather. I'm sure they thought it was like the messiah himself had risen from the grave to see them. For my part, I did my best to smile and tried to remember not to shake hands with my right, though inevitably I forgot and cracked some fingers. I would apologize, they would say that it was no problem and that they understood that I still hadn't recovered fully from my injuries, and the next of my fans would come up to meet me.

After three days of this siege, I was sick and tired of it all. Appropriately, that was when the opposition decided that they wanted to negotiate.

I received a message from Jakob stating that he would be sending one of his clones, along with three of the Guildmasters under his domain, to speak with me and my followers. He wanted to meet on "neutral ground" in the primary airlock doors separating the spaceport from the Marquez cavern. I told him that there was no such thing as neutral ground on this asteroid, and he may as well come out here to the bay. He agreed, but only on the condition that each of the representatives he was sending be allowed to bring a bodyguard. I told him that we would match each of these bodyguards one to one and if they brought too many, the negotiations would be called off immediately. With that, the meeting time was set for the following day shortly after noon.

On the day of the negotiations, we set up a large table in the middle of the cave, far enough away from the camp that it would take time for our people to run up and grab the negotiators, but close enough to give everyone in the camp a clear shot at everyone else. Handling negotiations on our side were me, Olga, and a horse by the name of Harvey, who seemed to be one of the organizers of our little militia. Denal was acting as one of our bodyguards. Somehow he'd gotten hold of another sword like the one that had snapped off in Derrick Marquez's bodysuit, but he kept it sheathed and carried a Gauss rifle loaded with armor-piercing flechettes. Clearly he had learned something, though I admit it wasn't much. Half an hour before the representatives were due to arrive, we sat down and awaited their arrival.

We waited almost two hours before they showed up. As they came, Denal and our other bodyguards held out portable IR, UV, and radar scanners to make sure they weren't accompanied by more than the four fully armored men we could see, as if they needed more. They were Jerome Marquez, Georgia Wolf, and a ram who went by the name of Nicholas Oak, all dressed in suits that I guessed concealed body armor, as well as a familiar-looking savannah cat dressed in the white robe of the SPPS hierarchy. A *very* familiar-looking savannah cat, I realized, as he sat down and shot me a small wink.

"Maximus!" I exclaimed in a moment of recognition.

"Yes. Father thought that you would be more inclined to trust the one of us you already knew best."

I looked around at the other negotiators. Olga and her mother were staring at one another with expressions of mutual disapproval, while Jerome Marquez was shooting

Denal a look that couldn't be interpreted as anything less than murderous intent. Harvey and Nicholas, on the other hand, seemed to be studying one another, attempting to guess one another's next move I supposed.

I turned back to the Griggs representative. "How can I be sure that you're really Maximus? There are, what, six of you? And Octavius helped your dad shoot me out into space and fried my subvocal comm."

Maximus withdrew at that accusation. "Seriously? We knew Dad gave him some help passing the entry exams but I didn't know he was assisting in executions." Noticing that everyone at the table had turned to stare at him, he cleared his throat and addressed my question. "Anyhow, I could remind you that you showed me the mutation in the promoter to MOR10X-6 in the first place. Or that I was the one who told you all that stuff about sexual reproduction's benefits and gave you the backup I'd made of the data Dad made you delete."

The others on his side of the table turned on him immediately. "You did that?!" Jerome Marquez sputtered. "You're the one who gave this creature the means to tear down the very foundations of the society we've worked so hard to build?!"

Olga threw in her own comment. "When the foundation is rotten, it needs to be torn down. And this society is founded on the worst form of government known to humanity."

Georgia Wolf leaned across the table to glower at her clone. "We have been working our hardest to treat our clients with the respect they deserve." She pointed to Denal. "We even took in that murderer when he gave us evidence that he had been framed."

Denal cowered behind his mate at this statement. Olga

only laughed at it. "Please. I know that you only decided to defend him in order to use him as a bargaining chip with Marquez at some point." I could see her rolling her eyes as she added. "And I've seen some of the stuff my sisters have gotten away with."

"So what does Jakob want?" I cut in, not particularly caring for this little family reunion that was interrupting the peace talks we so desperately wanted at this point.

"Right," Maximus started. "He wants you all off this rock." I just stared at him blankly for a few seconds. "He's chartered a fleet of passenger liners to move you and all your supporters to Ceres."

"An entire fleet?" I asked incredulously. "For just a few hundred of us? Sounds a bit expensive."

Nicholas Oak finally spoke up. "It's not just the small army you have gathered here. We're estimating that with all the rioters scattered across the asteroid and the non-violent followers of yours, there are possibly five thousand 'reproductionists,' as some of us have started to call them."

"Five. Thousand." I had no idea there were so many parahumans who believed me, much less that they were willing to fight for the right to use my invention.

"Yes," Maximus confirmed. "And Dad wants them all out of Vesta by the end of the week. So badly that he'll spend a small fortune to get them out of his way."

"Sounds like a very generous offer," I mused. "But I'm afraid I can't go to Ceres, as I'm sure you can recall why."

"Then go to Hygeia or something. I don't care so long as you're not interfering with our rule over these habitats." Marquez's statement seemed rather angry, but it sounded sincere, like he really thought that this was the best plan for dealing with us, which actually made me suspicious.

"We can order the ships to go anywhere within their range," Maximus stated. I perked up at the word "we." He seemed to notice, because he then said, "I'm coming with you."

He pulled at his SPPS robe and began to tear it off. "I no longer feel safe here," he said as he tossed the discarded robe to one of the bodyguards.

We stared in amazement as the now naked feline walked around the table to stand next to us, our own guards training their guns on him.

I turned back to the remaining Guild negotiators. "Tell Jakob we accept his offer." I moved to stand up, wincing a little as the hole in my side was forced to bend. "And I believe that concludes our meeting for today. Goodbye."

Georgia Wolf, Jerome Marquez, and Nicholas Oak gave us a last parting look of displeasure before getting up to leave. Once they were gone, Olga turned to Maximus. "What are you thinking?! You're a clone of Argen's sworn enemy entering a camp full of people who want to overthrow your father! How long do you think you'll survive here?!"

Max grimaced as he tried to formulate an answer. Finally he settled on this: "You're a clone of one of my dad's lapdogs. They seem to accept you just fine."

"They know that I'm HoundOfGod; they're well aware that I'm on their side," Olga responded rather emphatically. "And for the record, House Wolf has a reputation as one of the... the..." her gaze drifted downwards as she trailed off. Suddenly, she slammed her palm over her eyes and said. "Somebody give him some pants; that's very distracting."

At this command, Denal walked up behind his mate and put his arms around her possessively. A low hissing sound began to utter from his throat. Seeking to diffuse the situation, I undid my kilt and held it out to Maximus. Now everyone's eyes were on me instead. "It's not like I have anything to hide," I retorted. Then I moved to change the subject. "So, Max, what's the catch that you didn't want to talk about in front of the goons?"

As Maximus struggled to put on the kilt, he spoke again. "Well, they didn't tell me anything, but after seeing that video of yours, where he confessed to engineering my grand-progenitor's demise, I expected that he had somehow sabotaged the ships he chartered."

Harvey, Denal, and two of our bodyguards mouths dropped open in shock. I had expected as much though, and if Olga was surprised, she didn't show it.

"And what do you suggest we do about it?" I asked.

Max shrugged. "I do have quite a few qcoins in my personal wallet." He held up his wristpad, which, aside from my kilt, was the only thing he was wearing. "I might be able to purchase some old freighters and habitation modules to take us wherever we decide to go."

"Let me see," I said, and he pulled up the qcoin wallet on his pad. I read the number, and my eyes went wide open in shock. "This may be enough for the habitat modules and a down payment on a junker freighter to carry them. We would need a lot more to buy one outright. And it might be enough to transport 3,000 people."

"Well, how many ships do our supporters have?" Denal asked. "We might be able to cram a dozen people into our ship, and I think we have the capacity to haul enough modules for twenty more."

"At the moment," I said, "I'm more concerned about where we'd go. You and I cannot return to Ceres, and I get the feeling that these people will want to follow us wherever we go."

"How about Pallas?" We turned to Harvey. This was the first time we'd heard him speak since the negotiations began. "It's pretty close in size to Vesta, but there are no permanent settlements due to its erratic orbit. Any colonists would be cut off from the majority of the Belt for months at a time."

"But that happens to be what we want now isn't it?" I stated. "But how would we get there if there are no permanent settlements?"

"I own a small cargo hauler," Harvey replied. "I think I could transport maybe fifty people in habitat modules. And to answer your question, Denal, the people down here have at least partial ownership of maybe five mining ships like yours and eight cargo ships of various sizes. We could load them up with habitat modules, use the mining ships to land them on the surface of Pallas, and dig tunnels for more permanent habitation—or seal up the ones already dug by prospectors."

"You've thought this out, haven't you?" I suggested.

"Always helps to have an escape plan," the horse told us. "But if that sheep was telling the truth about there being nearly five thousand of us out there, we are going to need that freighter this clone was talking about." He pointed at Maximus.

I looked at Maximus as if expecting him to do something. Finally I told him, "Transfer the money to Olga. We're going shopping."

Chapter 16

We found a trans-system rated freighter older than me for a down payment of a mere one million qcoins, about half of what Maximus Griggs had given us. The dealer took some persuasion to give it to a bunch of "zealots who would be taking it far beyond any resemblance of civilized space," though. And to be fair, there was a decent chance that we wouldn't be able to make very many of the quarterly payments on it.

The habitat modules, equipped with cabins, carbon dioxide scrubbers, and algae tanks sufficient to support two to twenty people apiece, were much easier to acquire, though most of the ones we could find were intended for temporary mining camps rather than building a long-term settlement. Just to be safe, we also bought some inflatable air tanks to give us extra space to move around in once we got to the planetoid.

When Olga posted our plan online, we got over four thousand replies expressing interest in leaving with us. They brought another pair of mining ships and a trio of cargo ships with them. It took three days to find all the ships and equipment our little colony would need to get started, followed by another week to prepare it all for the journey. It was during this step that the first problems began to emerge.

Four days from our scheduled time of departure, I found myself and Olga in one of the maintenance crawlspaces on our "new" freighter while Denal showed us something he had spotted while certifying it as spaceworthy. The object was a small cube about ten centimeters to a side and welded onto one of the support struts. "What is it?" I asked.

"Cutting charge." Said Denal curtly. "At a pre-set time or a signal from a detonator it will send a blast of hot plasma through this beam and sever it neatly. Could cause the entire ship to fold in half if it blew during or before a burn. It might even look like normal wear and tear."

"And then we look fatally incompetent." I realized. "While he remains innocent in the public view."

"They sabotaged it this quickly?" Olga asked. "We've only had it a week! Who would have been able to put it in place?"

"I think I know," said Denal. "He may not have picked this one out, but Maximus was there when we bought it."

"It was his money we used," Olga objected. "He had the right to know what we were using it for."

"There you go again!" Denal swung himself towards his mate in the cramped space of the crawlway. "Ever since he joined us, you've been defending him every time I suggest that something's going on." He drew in right up against her face. "And don't think I haven't seen you sneaking peeks at his butt."

"Jealous?" Olga sniggered.

Exactly what was going on? It was starting to remind me of some human movie I'd seen a while ago, though exactly which one escaped my mind for a while. Then I registered a strange musky scent coming from the feuding couple, and they suddenly began to grapple with one another, bouncing around in the tiny space, banging into the walls. As I watched, I noticed their mouths attempting to close around one another's, biting each other's muzzles. Then I spotted Olga pulling Denal's dick out of his pants, and it clicked. "You two, what are you doing?!"

Both of them craned their necks to look back at me. "It's called a 'lover's spat' or something like that." Denal told me. "You'd know if you had any hormones."

"Would those hormones by any chance be making you possessive of Olga and Olga interested in other, more powerfully built males?" I suggested.

"What? I'm not attracted to Maximus!" Olga objected. This caused Denal to turn back to her and glower. "I get so hot when you act jealous," she continued, "so it's more your fault for setting me off like that."

The pheromones those two were giving off were starting to saturate the already stale air. It was starting to make me feel strange, like there was a tightness down where my genitals should have been, an itch I couldn't scratch. My breathing rate and heart beats increased and I felt my temperature rising. I had to get out of here quickly.

"Denal," I said, "find someone to help you remove this thing and look for others. Jakob didn't need Maximus; the sale was public record, and there were two days before we came into possession for him to get one of his stooges to plant bombs. Olga, don't put this on the nets until we've left. If I were Jakob and knew that the first plan failed I'd put a backup plan in place as quickly as possible." I then bent myself awkwardly to turn around and leave.

Leaving Denal and Olga's proximity didn't cause the effect of the pheromones they'd been producing to wear off as quickly as I wanted. In fact, I'm pretty sure that my fur and clothes were soaked in it. The flustered feeling persisted as I wound my way through the miniature canvas town set up in the spaceport down to the tent set up for Maximus Griggs. When I found him, he was lying on his inflated mattress, reading something on a tablet.

"'Men never do good unless necessity drives them to it; but when they are free to choose and can do just as they please, confusion and disorder become rampant'", he said, apparently reading out loud. He set aside the tablet as I bent down to enter his temporary domicile. "Maybe if the original colonists had read this, we could have avoided this whole situation."

I sat down next to him and picked up the tablet; it showed an image of what looked like yellowed parchment covered with a rather exotic font that I hadn't seen before. "Interesting choice of reading material," I commented.

"*Discourses on Livy*," Maximus explained. "Supposedly, it's about how to run a republic."

"A what?"

"I'm still trying to figure that out. I started out looking up human political literature but the books all contradicted one another. One said that capitalism was the driver of progress; another claimed that it was a tool of the upper class to oppress the workers." He shook his head in disgust. "I tried searching for an author who studied politics like it was a science instead of trying to forward some ideology, and it came up with an early sixteenth century Italian named Niccolò Machiavelli."

"Seriously? They haven't done a rigorous study of politics in nearly six hundred years?"

"Seriously," Max affirmed as he took the tablet back. "He wrote a much shorter book called *The Prince* that detailed how feudal principalities were run. If I hadn't known that my father wasn't allowed to consume any human media, I would have thought he read it."

"You are not making me a king," I said, shifting across the mattress towards him. "Or a queen for that matter. A crown wouldn't fit well with these ears." I held one pyramidal ear in my left hand and showed it to him.

"Well, this book seems to be a bit in favor of something closer to democracy. Look here." He pointed to the beginning of one paragraph. "'The demands of a free populace, too, are very seldom harmful to liberty, for they are due either to the populace being oppressed or to the suspicion that it is going to be oppressed...'"

"Well, then, you keep reading, and maybe we can set up one of these republics on Pallas." The depression in the air mattress sank down, and I found myself sliding closer to him. Unconsciously, my right hand apparently wandered in the direction of his crotch, because he jumped slightly in shock.

"Jeez, Argen!" he yelled at me. "Are you trying to castrate me or something?!"

I realized that my prosthetic hand, which I still had trouble controlling, was attempting to cup his testicles. I apologized and slowly withdrew the hand. "Would you rather have my normal hand?" I flipped over and shot my left hand down his pants.

"What is up with you?" he asked. "Ever since you came in, you've been acting like you're drunk or something." He sniffed my breath for traces of alcohol or other intoxicants.

"Oh." I suddenly remembered my whole justified–to

myself–reason for coming here. "Denal and Olga were fighting a bit over you. Denal seems to think you're trying to…" I trailed off. Even if Maximus wasn't still working for his father, there was a chance that if he knew about the bombs, Jakob would find out anyways. So I finished with, "…steal Olga from him. And Olga said that was ridiculous, but he was so hot when he got jealous. Apparently, the amount of pheromones they were giving off as they fought and started to have sex then and there was enough to affect even those of us without gonads."

"You do smell a bit like them," Max purred as he reached down towards my hand. I felt his cock swell and grow hard in my grasp.

"Feels like it's working on you, too." I moved to straddle him and began to unzip his pants.

"I have noticed that my sex drive seems to have increased since I took the mutagen." He started to help me remove his pants and pull them downwards. "If everyone out there is this horny, it could be a problem."

"We'll worry about that later." I then clamped my muzzle against his and thrust my tongue in. My hands guided his cock into my rectum.

"Wait." He forced me away for a second and spat in his hands, rubbed it around, and spread it over his penis. "Afraid I don't have any proper lubricant, but I think that might do for now."

"I didn't even know you needed lubrication," I commented with a bit of surprise. "Explains why it hurt so badly that time me and Denal tried it."

"Oh, so that panda has been in here, too?" he asked, grabbing onto my thighs and pulling it down onto him.

"Not for months now." I plunged down and felt his shaft bend a little as it slid deep inside my colon, rubbing abrasively against my inner walls, but this time the pain was mild enough that I could feel a bit of pleasure from the intrusion. I spread my arms down on either side of him to brace myself as I bounced up and down on him, both of us starting to moan in pleasure. Then he came to climax. I felt a spurt of something hot and sticky flood my bowels and he let out a scream of delight.

That was when the tent flap swung open and a militiaman pushed his way in brandishing a pistol. Caught off guard, I clenched the mattress with both hands. I heard a popping sound and a hiss of escaping air coming from near my right hand. I turned to glare at this intruder angrily.

"Oh, sorry," said the militia, an ursine whom I suspected had worked for one of the Protectors' Guilds. "I heard the scream and assumed something was wrong. Not the first time I made that mistake this week. Wait…" Then he finally seemed to recognize me and glanced around to my prosthetic hand which was still clamped around a torn piece of the mattress. "Aren't you the one who discovered the sterility gene?"

"If you mean Argentum then yes, I am." I withdrew my hand as the mattress sank lower and lower to the floor. "And I think you owe Maximus here a new air mattress." I showed him the cybernetic appendage, with pieces of plastic still stuck in the joints.

"Oh, sorry sir. I just thought I'd heard that you were a, a, um…"

"Neuter," I supplied. I then lifted myself off Maximus, letting his dick flop out, and lifted my kilt to show him my cum-stained derriere. "But that doesn't mean I lack fun holes."

"Right, right. I'll go get a replacement mattress right

away. Would you like anything else? Some lube perhaps?"

"Forget it; you killed the mood." I waved him away and he left. I then flopped down next to Maximus on the still deflating mattress, pushing it all the way down to the hard cave floor.

Maximus turned to me and began to speak again. "You ever consider getting a bioprinted hand to replace that thing?" he asked, gesturing towards my prosthesis.

I held the hand up, looked at it, rotated the wrist, and opened and closed the fingers multiple times, getting the timing wrong and causing my index and thumb to collide on several of those attempts. "It would take over a month for my nerves to grow into a biological transplant," I finally said. "And even more time to relearn how to use it. I may not have full control over this thing yet, but it's better than lugging around a completely numb and useless thing on the end of my arm."

"Well, what about sex organs? Have you considered getting a vagina, or a penis?" He felt under my skirt and rubbed the featureless surface of my crotch.

"You wouldn't mind a penis?" I asked him. "Even if I wanted to use it from time to time?"

"Well, we wouldn't be able to have kids anyways, so why should it matter? I'm not too sure about having a cock up my butt from time to time, but maybe we could try something like that. I saw what looked like some prosthetic plastic penises in one of the sex aid product booths they have set up out there."

Ah, yes. The sex shops had popped up shortly after the first few tents. Apparently some of the capitalists out there in the rest of the asteroid had figured that a group of people who had just become fertile would be screwing one another a lot. From what I'd seen, they did indeed have a lot of business. It was at that moment that the bear who had barged in before chose to rap on the tent flap.

Both of us got up and unzipped the flap to see him. He was holding a small inflatable mattress, like he had promised. Maximus took it and moved back to set it up. Now that the guard had a good look at his face, he said. "Aren't you that clone of the guy who runs the SPPS?"

"Yes, his name is Maximus, and we knew one another at work," I told him curtly. "Now why don't you go down to one of the sex booths and pick up some lube and one of those fake dicks?"

"Uh, right," he said, a bit flustered. "What size were you thinking?"

"Small!" was Max's response, with a bit of fear in his voice.

"As if I'd get a minuscule cock," I said in reply. Then turning back to the bear outside, I said, "Medium."

"Right, then. I'll go get those." The militiaman turned around and left, still looking a bit flustered.

I closed the flap again and went back to my boyfriend, now laying out the new mattress and attaching the pump to start inflating. He looked at me and smiled a bit, not showing as many teeth as his father's scary grins. "You realize that he'll tell all his friends at the booze tents that their prophet was seduced by the enemy's son?"

I lay down on my belly and flicked my tail playfully at him. "So shall I get the story straight when he comes back and tell him that I seduced you?"

Chapter 17

The day of the launch had arrived. Denal's team had removed five different charges from various points along the superstructure of our primary colony ship and hidden them in a warehouse maintained by Clan Marquez. The habitat modules, like giant crates, were attached to the superstructure, and pressurized access tubes were set up so that people could float from module to module without exposing themselves to vacuum. As we prepared to set off, I stood on the bridge of the massive freighter and watched as people filed into the ship and spread throughout its cargo holds. Others chose to board the numerous smaller ships that would also be making the journey. They took off one by one. So many out there, all willing to come simply because I had offered to give them children. Who would have thought?

Harvey was flying his own ship. Denal and Olga were on board our old vessel carrying two habitat modules on tow cables. I had been offered the captain's cabin on board the freighter and had been advised to take it so as to not seem ungrateful. Since it seemed like a waste of space for just one person, though, I would share it with Maximus, who now hid among the crowd currently gathered on the bridge.

Once our mothership, as I suppose you could call it, was fully loaded and ready to depart, I was apparently expected to give some kind of speech, judging by the camera minidrones that suddenly began to circle around me. I've seen the video; it was not particularly flattering compared to some of my other streamed appearances. I just stood there for three minutes, looking nervous, until I worked up the courage to say something.

"Today, we set out to build a new life for ourselves. We go not only to colonize a new planetoid but also to build the foundation of a new future for all parahumanity." To be honest, I was starting to grasp at straws at that point. "We will build a society where parahumans are not dependent on the whims of petty wanna-be tyrants to reproduce."

I looked around. Everyone was still staring at me like they were expecting more. "That's it. What do you expect? I'm a scientist, not a politician."

That last sentence was greeted by a chorus of laughter and applause. I hadn't really intended to make a joke, but that seemed to be how it was being received. Freaking anarchists.

I went over to my seat in the captain's chair and strapped myself down. The others either found seats or went to their cabins to strap themselves down in their provided crash couches. I noticed Maximus heading up to the crew quarters.

Well over ten minutes later, the docking clamps let loose and the thrusters started up, moving us slowly away from Vesta. It took more than an hour after that before we were far enough away to start up the fusion torch drive. Then I felt the familiar rush of acceleration as we went into burn. At that point I decided it was time to head back to my cabin. I let myself loose and grabbed onto the ladder that had just sprung out of the floor, letting myself down to the "floor" that was a wall just a couple hours ago. I climbed down until I got to the crew deck and got off. They were oriented so that acceleration would act like gravity. My cabin was all the way down at the end of a hallway. I was able to simply walk down. Maximus was already there.

"You have any trouble finding the place?" I asked him as I sat down next to him.

"One of the self-appointed security guys tried to tell me I was in the wrong section," Maximus started. "But then one of the other crew told him that I was your boy toy or something. He let me go right away."

I groaned as I leaned back, "I'll need to talk to the crew about a lot of things. Like not holding up launch an extra fifteen minutes crowding the bridge just so they can hear me make a speech I wasn't expecting to make."

"It's weird, isn't it, this treatment like you're some kind of revolutionary leader when all you did was rediscover a gene?" He leaned back to match my eye level. "I've been reading some more of the *Discourses* and on the specific government that they primarily talk about."

"Really now. Why don't you tell me about it?"

"Well, it's about Rome, which was a republic for almost five hundred years before they elected a dictator named Julius Caesar, who turned it into an empire that conquered most of Europe and northern Africa and reigned for another four hundred years before it split…"

We were about a week out when the first signs of trouble appeared. A news report from Vesta stated that a warehouse at the spaceport had exploded. Jakob Griggs was blaming "Reproducers" or whatever the current term they were using for our "movement" was. I called a meeting with the captains of the various ships of the fleet via secure laser-line communications.

An entire wall of my cabin was composed of a massive LCD monitor. I set it to display the images of every other influential person in our improvised fleet. My own image would be transmitted for everyone else to see via a tiny camera embedded just above the monitor.

I addressed Denal specifically, "I think it's time you told everyone what you found."

Denal shrugged and looked to Olga nervously, as if waiting for her approval. She nodded. He turned back to the camera and let out a long breath before speaking. "A few days before we left, I found cutting charges attached to various points along the superstructure of our freighter. I removed them and left them in one of the warehouses at the dock." He slumped forward in his seat. "I honestly expected them to find those things long ago."

Objections and complaints erupted from the other captains:

"Why did you keep this secret?!"

"What did you think was going to happen?!"

"That was the signal, damn it!"

"Wait, what was that?" I called out at the last statement. I noticed that one of the captains, a weasel or something, had disappeared, leaving a blank screen with just the words "signal lost" in the place of his image. "Where did he go?"

"Oh shit!" Harvey exclaimed. "The *Defiant* just broke laser-line contact and jettisoned their habitat modules."

I opened an intercom to the bridge crew. "Send me a

feed of the sensor read-outs to my monitor."

In seconds, the images of the other captains were replaced with a radar map with labeled dots indicating the ships of the fleet and other nearby objects. One dot, labeled "Defiant", was racing towards the freighter.

"Give me all readouts! I was a prospector, you know. Direct deep penetrating radar and radiation sensors at the *Defiant!*"

As I watched the display, fuzzy clouds of different colors and densities indicating types and intensities of radiation appeared around the ships of the fleet. Most of the ships had a faint cloud of red for infrared tinted with some gamma green if their reactors had faulty containment. A window opened, showing the mass profile of the *Defiant*. It was a fairly standard, medium-sized transport, though the hull around the cargo bay was unusually dense–that was typically the lightest armored part of a ship, given how there were rarely any living organisms transported in those compartments.

I didn't have long to wonder about that unusual design before the reason became apparent, and violently. A pair of panels on the front of the cargo compartment flew off and a couple of very fast-moving green dots shot out. The nuclear missiles locked onto a pair of ships that lay between us and the *Defiant*. One ship managed to shoot down the missile after it. The other was not so lucky. There was a multicolored burst on the radiation scanners, and the ship was simply gone.

"Get a message off to the rest of the fleet!" I ordered.

"We can't!" was the strained reply. "There's too much interference from the radiation!"

"Damn, damn, damn!" I said to myself. We had minimal weapons and no way to signal the other ships to fire upon the aggressor.

But slowly, the others seemed to get the idea. They poured their point-defense weapons onto the *Defiant*.

Unfortunately, it seemed to do nothing. They were apparently much better armored than the pirate we had seen off Ceres.

One ship, Denal and Olga's, even launched a missile. I did not know they had installed a missile launcher, but I was a bit relieved until their missile flew past the *Defiant* while that ship fired its own missiles at our freighter. Were they working for Jakob, too?

But then the missile fired by Olga and Denal arced between the *Defiant* and its own missiles. There was a flash, and when the scanners were clear again, the *Defiant*'s fore was partially melted and scarred as if by a barrage of lasers, and its missiles were tumbling out of control.

"What the hell was that?!" I shouted.

"I think it was an x-ray laser warhead," said one of the bridge crew. "They're often used to intercept missiles, but they're expensive. Where would they get one of those?"

We didn't have much time to speculate as the *Defiant* began to accelerate straight forward on an impact course with us.

"Move us out of the way! Shoot them down! Do something!" I commanded.

The ship bucked to one side as the thrusters kicked in and then pushed me down into the flight couch as the fusion torch went full throttle. On the screen, I watched as our coilguns loosed volley after volley of slugs into them. But still the mutinous vessel careened onward. Ten kilometers, seven kilometers, four kilometers, two kilometers, half a kilometer...

And then it went straight past us. The cameras and

coilguns rotated to follow the *Defiant*, but before they could do anything more, it exploded. Debris flew outwards from the blast, but our coilguns knocked the larger chunks out of our way.

"What," I gasped, "was that?!"

"The lasers must have taken out their sensors," suggested someone on the bridge. "Not sure why they blew up, though. I didn't think we hit them that hard."

"Suicide attackers," I said. What had Jakob offered them to inspire such loyalty? What did he have that would be any good to them when they were dead? Clones? Assurance of their genetic immortality? We would have to do something about that.

As we passed out of the radiation cloud, the scanners began to pick up the rest of the fleet. What I saw stunned me: There was a dogfight going on at the far side of the formation. Or rather, three ships were firing upon a fourth that was trying to weave between their shots. I grabbed at the icon for the ship being pursued, and an information tag came up.

It was Denal and Olga's ship.

I spoke into the intercom again. "Do we have communications back?"

"Half of the radio frequencies are clear again. Do you wish to speak to someone?"

"Yes. Message to all ships: This is Argentum; cease fire immediately! I repeat: Cease fire!"

The message had been out for less than a minute before the bridge crew came calling back. "Receiving response."

"Let's hear it."

"Not all the traitors are dead. You may have missed it, but this one launched a nuke in your direction."

"Send response: I did see the laser warhead that destroyed the *Defiant's* nukes and blinded them so that their attempt at ramming failed. Stand down. We will handle this."

Grudgingly, the three aggressor ships broke off their pursuit. I radioed Denal and Olga to ascertain their well-being.

"Hey, Silver, the hull was a little pitted but I don't think we sustained any major damage." Denal's voice said over the radio channel. I let out a small sigh of relief.

But then I heard some faint chattering coming over the band, like someone else on his ship was speaking to him. "What? Are you sure? Oh no. Oh no. Get someone out there to check for survivors! Oh, sorry, this is still on. One of our exterior habitat modules was ruptured."

I swear I could hear the joints in my cyborg hand start to crack.

Chapter 18

Two months had passed since the incident with the *Defiant*. We had continued despite our losses and were now in orbit over our prize, 2 Pallas. It hung below us, a cratered orb like the one our group had fled so recently—two, in my and Denal's case. But since it lacked the sprawling surface factories and spaceports that covered the surfaces of Ceres and Vesta, the only detectable signs of habitation here were the skeletal remains of abandoned mining camps. The survey probes indicated that the planetoid's carbonaceous resources were largely untouched, but the life-giving ice had largely been mined out. We ended up picking a spot far from most of the mining sites, low in metals, but we could send ships to gather them. The plans for the settlement were drawn up, landing sequences were organized, and then they just stood there.

I looked around the bridge from my chair in the center of the room. Everyone was staring at me. Maximus Griggs leaned over and whispered in my ear. "They're waiting, hon."

I waved him away and stared directly at the center of the main viewscreen. "Go ahead," I told the fleet. "You all know the plan. You can begin landing."

The mining ships that could actually land on the surface of an asteroid without a docking cradle began firing retro-rockets to bring their habitat modules down to Pallas. There they would detach and drill anchors into the surface. Once the craft had lifted off again, people in the habitats would start stringing up crawl tubes between the modules. As more modules were brought down to the surface, the settlement would be laid down in a spiral pattern, with each habitat connected to its immediate neighbors in the same "arm" and adjacent ones. A bit of a hassle to move from one end of the colony to another, but it would do until we'd excavated a cave underground.

"Finally, it's all over," I said as I slumped down in my chair. "Just asteroid mining from now on. I can handle that."

"I wouldn't be too sure about that," the cat by my side told me. "There's so much that needs to be done. We are, after all, building a whole civilization out here."

"And you and Olga seem to have a better idea of how civilizations should be run than I do," I told Maximus.

"And you expect them to follow us? I'm the clone of their worst enemy, and she's the progeny of one of his cronies. You, on the other hand, they seem to adore as their savior."

"Do you think I want to be worshipped? I'd much rather go back to shining light at powdered rocks."

He drew himself towards me, sprawling over my lap and looking up at me with those pleading wide eyes. "There's nearly four thousand people out there. What's stopping another demagogue like my father from taking over? They're used to anarchic feudalism. What if another tragedy like that one just a few weeks ago occurs? So many deaths that you could help us prevent."

"All right, all right!" I groaned, shoving him off and getting up. "Fine, I'll be your king or queen or messiah or whatever." I pointed at him with most of the fingers on my right hand, still having difficulty selectively extending them. "Just promise me that the instant you no longer need me, I can go back to the rock crushing."

Maximus Griggs struggled to right himself in the virtually nil gravity. Once he was done, he stood up as straight as possible. "I promise."

You know, I never did get back to that spectrophotometer.

www.ingramcontent.com/pod-product-compliance
Lightning Source LLC
Chambersburg PA
CBHW051521170626
46811CB00002B/934